Also by Alex Morgan:

THE KICKS SERIES

SAVING THE TEAM

SABOTAGE SEASON

WIN OR LOSE

HAT TRICK

SHAKEN UP

UNDER PRESSURE

BREAKAWAY: BEYOND THE GOAL

ALEX MORGAN

Simon & Schuster Books for Young Readers
New York   London   Toronto   Sydney   New Delhi

SIMON & SCHUSTER BOOKS FOR YOUNG READERS
An imprint of Simon & Schuster Children's Publishing Division
1230 Avenue of the Americas, New York, New York 10020
This book is a work of fiction. Any references to historical events, real people, or real places are used fictitiously. Other names, characters, places, and events are products of the author's imagination, and any resemblance to actual events or places or persons, living or dead, is entirely coincidental.
Text copyright © 2016 by Full Fathom Five, LLC, and Alex Morgan
Cover illustrations copyright © 2016 by Paula Franco
All rights reserved, including the right of reproduction in whole or in part in any form.
SIMON & SCHUSTER BOOKS FOR YOUNG READERS
is a trademark of Simon & Schuster, Inc.
For information about special discounts for bulk purchases, please contact Simon & Schuster Special Sales at 1-866-506-1949 or business@simonandschuster.com.
The Simon & Schuster Speakers Bureau can bring authors to your live event. For more information or to book an event, contact the Simon & Schuster Speakers Bureau at 1-866-248-3049 or visit our website at www.simonspeakers.com.
Also available in a Simon & Schuster Books for Young Readers hardcover edition
Book design by Krista Vossen
The text for this book was set in Berling.
Manufactured in the United States of America
0217 OFF
First Simon & Schuster Books for Young Readers paperback edition March 2017
2 4 6 8 10 9 7 5 3 1
The Library of Congress has cataloged the hardcover edition as follows:
Names: Morgan, Alex (Alexandra Patricia), 1989– author.
Title: Settle the score / Alex Morgan.
Description: First edition. | New York : Simon & Schuster Books for Young Readers, [2016] | Series: The Kicks ; [6] | Summary: Playing on different teams during winter league soccer tests the friendship of a close-knit group of twelve-year-old girls.
Identifiers: LCCN 2015026691
ISBN 9781481451048 (hardback) | ISBN 9781481451055 (paperback)
ISBN 9781481451062 (ebook)
Subjects: | CYAC: Soccer—Fiction. | Friendship—Fiction. | BISAC: JUVENILE FICTION / Sports & Recreation / Soccer. | JUVENILE FICTION / Girls & Women. | JUVENILE FICTION / Social Issues / Friendship. Classification: LCC PZ7.M818 Se 2016 | DDC [Fic]—dc23
LC record available at http://lccn.loc.gov/2015026691

TO MY HUSBAND

CHAPTER ONE

"Noooooooooooooooooooooo!" Jessi yelled. I groaned with disappointment. The two of us sat together, watching a boys' winter league soccer game. Our friend Cody, on the Spartans, had taken a shot at the goal. It had gone high and to the left, looking like it would sail way over the goalie's head. But the goalie had jumped up and made a spectacular save.

The Wildcats fans in the stands cheered. But for the players on the field, there was no time to dwell on successes or losses. You had to constantly move and run your next play. I knew this very well. Both Jessi and I were playing for the girls' winter league, on a team called the Griffons. During the regular season we played soccer for the Kentville Kangaroos, or the Kicks, as most people called us.

That was the nice thing about living in California. I

could play soccer all year round if I wanted to. Which was fine with me, because I lived and breathed soccer. I even dreamed about it!

"Oh, the tragedy!" Frida moaned theatrically. "It was not to be."

"They're still ahead by one!" Emma reminded her, cheerful as always.

"Frida can turn anything into a drama," Jessi said, smiling at her. "I don't know why you aren't on *The Real Teenagers of Beverly Hills*!"

I laughed when Jessi mentioned the silly reality show she had gotten me hooked on. "Because as dramatic as Frida is, she's way too nice!" I said.

"But I bet it would be really fun to play the villain," Frida said, looking thoughtful. She was an actress. In fact, she had recently filmed a TV movie. When I'd lived in Connecticut, I hadn't known anyone who was a professional actor. But here things were different. It was pretty exciting having a friend who was starring in a movie.

I kept my eye on the soccer field as we talked. Our friend Steven on the Spartans stole the ball from the Wildcats and passed it to Cody. Cody took another shot at the goal, feigning left before kicking it hard and low to the right. The goalie went left, and the ball hit the lower right corner of the net. Goal!

As we cheered, Jessi smiled at me. "I'm glad we didn't have practice today, so we could be here at the game."

"I wish we could do both," I said. "The Griffons could

use some extra practice if we want to make it into the semifinals."

Emma chimed in. "Well, I'm glad you're here, and I'm glad Maisie's team didn't have practice either. This is fun."

Emma and Frida helped my dad coach my sister's elementary school soccer team. During the regular season they both played on the Kicks with me, Jessi, and our friend Zoe. Frida hadn't tried out for the winter league because she'd been filming her movie. Emma, who was an awesome goalie for the Kicks, had had a disastrous tryout and didn't make a winter league team. Zoe had, but not the Griffons. She was playing for the Gators instead.

"I know Zoe wanted to be here too," Emma continued, "but the Gators coach called for an extra practice. They really have their eye on the championship."

I looked at Jessi, my face creasing with worry. We really wanted to be winter league champions too. Why hadn't Coach Darby called an extra practice?

To be the champs we'd probably have to beat the Gators—which meant beating Zoe. Also, some of the other Kicks were on the Gators with her, including Grace, my Kicks co-captain. The idea of playing against my friends was throwing me off a bit, and that was the last thing I needed. Not too long before, an earthquake had shaken me up, and it had taken a while for me to get back my confidence. I didn't want to lose it again!

"Aren't you playing the Gators this Saturday?" Frida asked with her eyebrow arched. "Talk about drama!"

"No worries! There are no friends on the soccer field, just players on opposing teams," Jessi said with confidence. "Zoe will just have to understand when the Griffons wipe the field with the Gators!"

Now it was Emma's and Frida's turn to look worried.

"Oh my gosh, I just realized—who are we supposed to root for?" Emma asked. "The Griffons or the Gators? I mean, I was going to make a sign and everything, but now I don't know who to put on it!"

"Well, if you just put a big G on it, you'll be covered," Jessi joked.

"But a pink G for Griffons, or a purple G for Gators?" Emma asked, sounding really worried.

I felt so bad for poor Emma that even though I was just as worried, I acted like it didn't bother me.

"Don't even make a sign," I told her. "Just cheer whenever you want. We know you love us equally. And pretty soon this will all be over and we'll all be back on the Kicks."

Emma smiled. "I can't wait for that!"

Pretending not to be worried actually helped as I turned the situation over in my head. *This is soccer*, I reminded myself. *Someone wins and someone loses. That's just how the game goes.* Whatever happened, I knew there was no way it would make things weird between me and my friends. Right?

But before I could dwell on it any more, the whistle blew and the game ended. The Spartans were the winners, 3–1.

Emma's and Frida's rides were waiting in the parking lot. We said good-bye as I checked the time on my phone. My mom wouldn't be there for another twenty minutes, and we were giving Jessi a lift home.

"Do we have time to congratulate Cody and Steven?" she asked.

I grinned. "Yep!"

Now, when I said that Cody and Steven were *our* friends, that was true. But it might have been a little truer to say that Cody and Jessi were friends, and Steven and I were friends—friends who really liked each other. Don't get me wrong. Steven and I weren't boyfriend and girlfriend or anything like that. After all, we were all only in the seventh grade. And I was pretty sure that my parents wouldn't let me go out on an actual date until I was around thirty-five years old. But Steven did have a supercute smile, and sometimes, when he flashed it at me, I felt the butterflies begin to dance in my stomach.

"Hey, congrats!" Jessi shouted to Cody as we walked onto the field. The rest of the Spartans were heading home, but Cody was still standing there, his hands on his hips and one foot resting on a soccer ball, while he talked to Steven.

As Cody looked up and smiled at her, Jessi raced over and kicked the soccer ball out from underneath his foot.

"Impressive goal out there, but let me show you how it's done!" Jessi called over her shoulder as she raced down the field with the ball.

Cody wobbled for a second before regaining his balance and tearing after Jessi.

Steven smiled at me, and I felt the butterflies start their cha-cha. He had short, dark hair that he stuck up a little with gel, but after the game it was more sweaty than spiky. That was okay with me. He still looked cute.

"Great game," I told him. "That was some interception."

"Thanks," he said, and I thought I saw a slight blush creep up his cheeks. Was Steven embarrassed because I'd complimented him? I felt a little awkward, not sure of what to say, until Jessi saved the day.

"Devin! I need backup!" she yelled from down the field as she tried to keep the ball away from Cody.

"Bro! Come help me out!" Cody called to Steven.

Steven grinned at me and shrugged his shoulders. "Those two are so hyper," he said.

"Well, if you can't beat 'em, join 'em." I smiled at him before racing away to receive a pass from Jessi.

Steven yelled as he ran after me, trying to steal the ball. All four of us kicked it back and forth for a while, laughing and messing around, while we tried to score on one another.

I was feeling so happy that any worries I'd had about playing the Gators had disappeared. I had my soccer mojo back and was ready for anything. Especially for the Griffons to win the winter league championship, no matter who I had to beat to do it. Game on!

CHAPTER TWO

"So then Addison went to the party as Taylor's brother's date, and Taylor flipped out," Jessi told me as we walked to the cafeteria the next day at school.

I gasped. "No way! What did Taylor do?"

"She smashed a piece of birthday cake into Addison's face!" Jessi sounded shocked, but then she started cracking up. "And then Addison's dog started licking it off."

I shook my head. Thankfully, these weren't people we actually knew. They were the stars of *The Real Teenagers of Beverly Hills*. I had missed last week's episode, and Jessi was filling me in.

"I wonder if Zoe's seen it yet," I said. Out of all of my friends, Zoe was definitely the most into fashion. She tuned in mostly to see what the girls were wearing, but like us, she couldn't help getting sucked into the silly drama.

"We'll ask her at lunch," Jessi said as we turned toward the double doors leading into the cafeteria.

Zoe was standing there, waiting for us.

"Hey, guys," she said with her usual shy smile. "So, um, I just wanted to let you know that today I'm going to sit with Grace and Anjali."

Grace and Anjali were Kicks too, but in the winter league they were on the Gators with Zoe.

"Gonna talk strategy for Saturday's game, huh?" Jessi teased her.

Zoe's eyes darted nervously around the hallway, not making eye contact with either of us. "Um, maybe a little bit," she said softly. "So, see you later?"

Before we could answer her, she turned and jogged off into the cafeteria.

Jessi looked at me and shrugged. "Pregame jitters?"

I shrugged back. Zoe had been acting a little odd. "I guess."

As we walked into the cafeteria, Emma waved at us from the table she was sitting at that was filled with members of the Tree Huggers, Kentville Middle School's environmental club.

We waved back and kept walking, looking for a table in the crowded cafeteria. Then we heard Frida's voice booming out from another table. "And then I told him he was blocking my light!" she said as her drama club friends laughed loudly.

Most days Jessi, Emma, Frida, Zoe, and I all sat together

at lunch, but sometimes we split up. Today was one of those days.

"Devin!" I heard a voice yell my name. I looked up and spotted Steven at a corner table, waving me over. He was sitting with Cody.

"Hey," I said as I slipped off my backpack and sat next to Steven. Jessi sat across from me. I pulled my lunch out of my backpack. Jessi was doing the same.

"So, how's the pizza today?" I asked. Both of the boys had cafeteria trays in front of them with half-eaten slices.

"Just like my mamma makes," Cody said in a really corny, fake Italian accent. Steven and I cracked up, but I noticed Jessi was frowning, lost in thought.

"Jessi, what's up?" I asked, worried. She loved Cody's silly jokes, so for her not to have a reaction was weird.

She let out a sigh. "Should we be strategizing too? Zoe is, and so are Grace and Anjali. The game is in two days. I want to win!"

"Are you playing the Gators on Saturday?" Steven asked.

I nodded. "Yes, and if we beat the Gators, we'll be guaranteed a spot in the semifinals. If we lose, we still get another chance. But why leave things to chance? We need to win!"

"You'll win," Steven said confidently. He always complimented me on my soccer skills. Now it was my turn to feel my cheeks blush.

"But what if you don't?" Cody asked. Jessi shot him an

angry look. He held his hands up in the air. "Aren't the Gators good too? It could be anyone's game."

Cody was right. The Gators *were* good. "Yeah, our record is pretty solid, but we had a loss to the Gazelles early on. If we lose against the Gators, the only other chance we'll have to make the semifinals will be our last regular season game against the Giraffes," I explained.

"Zoe is talking strategy right now, and her coach called an extra practice," Jessi said. She sounded stressed. "Demolition Darby needs to kick it into high gear!"

Jessi had nicknamed Coach Darby, the Griffons coach, Demolition Darby. Coach had a strict, no-nonsense approach to coaching. At first that had been hard for me to get used to. But I had been learning a lot from her about how to be more assertive on the field.

My thoughts drifted back to Zoe. She had definitely been acting weird around me and Jessi, and it was probably because she really wanted to beat us! And because we were friends, she felt uncomfortable about it. I wanted to win as much as Zoe did. But one of us was going to have to lose.

I sighed. "This is too strange, wanting to totally destroy your good friend's team!"

Cody shrugged. "That's soccer. It's a small world, at least around here. You get to know most of the players. We're playing against some of our Kangaroos on Sunday too."

"And after we slaughter them, we'll be moving to the semifinals!" Steven joked. He didn't look worried at all to be playing against his friends, and neither did Cody.

Jessi nodded. "I guess all we can do is focus on playing our best at Saturday's game. That's what the Gators are going to do. We can't worry about anything else. This is soccer, and it's how the game goes."

"Yeah, you're right," I agreed. I felt better as I began to eat my sandwich, grilled chicken with avocado that my mom had made for me.

Just then Hailey, a new student at Kentville Middle School, stopped by our table. Jessi glanced over at me. I knew what she was thinking. When Hailey had first come to school, Steven had spent a lot of time showing her around. Time he normally would have spent with me. It had gotten pretty awkward, and I had even wondered if Steven and I were no longer friends. But once I'd worked up the courage to talk to him about it, everything had gotten straightened out. And now I was starting to get to know Hailey for myself. She was really nice.

"Hi!" she said cheerfully. Hailey had curly brown hair and a big smile. "So," she said, looking to me and Jessi. "I know the winter league is winding down. Tryouts are right around the corner for the spring Kicks soccer season. Do you have any pointers? I really want to make the team."

Jessi laughed. "Don't worry. All you have to do is show up. Coach Flores is a total sweetie. She doesn't say no to anyone who really wants to play."

I nodded in agreement. Our Kicks coach was the total opposite of our Griffons coach.

"She wants to give everyone a chance," I told Hailey. "But if you want, I'd be happy to kick the ball around with you before tryouts. We can go over some of the drills that Coach Flores likes to run."

Hailey nodded. "That would be great, Devin. Thanks! I really want to be one of the Kicks."

"We'd really like to have you on the Kicks too," I said to Hailey, and I meant it. She seemed superfriendly and really excited to play soccer.

Steven looked up at the clock. "Oh man! Emmet's giving us another quiz today, right? I meant to study during lunch."

"I studied last night," I told him. After the earthquake, I had failed one of Mr. Emmet's World Civ quizzes, and I was not going to let that happen again! "We've got ten minutes left. I can help you."

"Thanks, Devin," Steven said, giving me the sweetest smile, and my heart did a little flip-flop. For the next ten minutes I didn't think about soccer at all, just ancient trade routes and how when the sun hit Steven's eyes, it looked like they were flecked with gold. Those ten minutes went really fast!

CHAPTER THREE

"Faster! Faster! You'll never be champions at this pace!"

I furiously dribbled the ball down the field, zigzagging between the cones set up for practice. Even though I had my hair pulled back into a ponytail, sweat was starting to pour down my forehead and run into my eyes. I hated when that happened!

A few hours before, I had worried that Coach Darby wasn't making us work hard enough. But boy, was I wrong. She was in full Demolition Darby mode. We'd been drilling at a breakneck pace for almost an hour now.

"Everybody drop where you are and give me twenty!" she called out, and we all fell to our knees as quickly as we could. My arms strained from the sixty push-ups we had already done today, but I gritted my teeth and did twenty more. I could hear a couple of the girls groaning, but I kept quiet. If Coach Darby even suspected you were weak, she would keep you on the bench. I had been benched by Darby before, and I was done with that. I wanted to play.

"Eight laps around the track!" Darby barked, and some of the groans got louder. This was the hardest she'd ever pushed us.

I jogged to the track, and one of my teammates, Katie, accidentally bumped into me from behind.

"Sorry!" she said, and she was smiling. "Darby's on fire today, right?"

"Yeah," I said, smiling back.

"She's burning up," said Mirabelle, jogging up behind me. "But so are we!"

She held up her hand, and we high-fived. Then the other girls started high-fiving one another as they jogged. Darby was being supertough, but nobody was giving in.

I couldn't believe it. When I'd first joined the Griffons, we'd had no team spirit. Everybody had been really competitive—it had been every player for herself. That was why we had lost our first game. Then Jessi and I had started doing some team building exercises, and once Coach Darby had seen that we played better as a result, she'd let us keep doing them.

It had kind of felt like a miracle. After all, we were on a team with Mirabelle, who was a member of the Pinewood team, the Kicks' biggest rival. We'd had some issues with Mirabelle before, but now she was someone I could call a friend. Not a close friend, but a friend.

But things weren't perfect. There was one teammate

who didn't want anything to do with team building, or even being nice: Jamie of the Riverdale Rams. During the Kicks' regular season she had actually tried to sabotage the Kicks so that we would lose! Jessi and I had been pretty upset when we'd ended up on a winter league team with Jamie. Even though we had put the sabotage behind us, it was hard to be on a team with someone who had no team spirit and hogged the ball whenever she could.

Even as we jogged around the track, Jamie didn't participate in the spontaneous high-fiving. She kept her eyes straight ahead. Her blond hair bounced in a ponytail against her neck as she ran, barely breaking a sweat.

There must be ice running through her veins, I thought, which felt a little mean, but it was a pretty honest description of Jamie. I had even tried being nice to her, but she hadn't warmed up to me at all.

By the time I finished the eighth lap, my legs were starting to feel like jelly. It was a relief when Coach Darby blew her whistle.

"Gather round!" she called out.

All eighteen Griffons jogged up to Coach Darby. The last rays of the afternoon sun cast an orange glow on her spiky blond hair.

"I want to see everyone here at noon on Saturday," she said. "One second late, and you'll be sitting on the bench. Got it?"

We all nodded.

"Get plenty of sleep the night before. No texting your

friends all night, or whatever it is you do that makes you all look so tired in the morning. We need to win this game on Saturday. We *can* win this game on Saturday. But the Gators are undefeated. We've got to give them all we've got. Do you hear me?"

"Yes, Coach!" we all shouted.

"Good," she said. "See you Saturday!"

Then everyone started milling around. Some girls were stretching, while others collapsed onto the grass.

"Hey, everybody, I was thinking we could go out for pizza on Saturday after the game," I said. "Win or lose."

"Who says we're going to lose?" Jessi asked.

"You know what I mean," I said. "We haven't gone out as a team in a while. I just thought it might be nice."

"It's a good idea, but does it have to be pizza, again?" Kristin asked.

"Yeah, but it's our tradition!" Zarine pointed out.

The other girls had started chiming in, saying they'd do it, and pizza was okay, when I noticed that Jamie was headed out to the parking lot.

"Be right back," I told my other teammates as I walked over to Jamie.

As I approached her, Jamie rolled her eyes, and I knew what she was thinking. Why was I even bothering? But even though Jamie might have been made of ice, I kept thinking I might be able to thaw her out somehow. She was the only player keeping us from having complete team unity. And that was something I really wanted. But besides that, I kind of felt sorry for Jamie. She didn't seem to have any real friends on the team, and it made her an outsider. I could at least try to make her feel included.

"Hey, Jamie!" I said. "I was just making plans with everybody to go out for pizza after the game on Saturday."

"How nice for you," she said, in that sarcastic way of hers. Her eyes darted around the parking lot, ignoring me.

"Well, it will be nice," I said, "and it would also be nice if you came with us."

Now, I'm sure I sounded like a dork. But I wasn't going to get caught up in being sarcastic back to Jamie. That was her game, not mine.

To my surprise Jamie turned to look at me. "Yeah, well, thanks for asking," she said. "I'm just not into celebrating, I guess. Not for myself, anyway." And then she walked away without another word.

That was a strange comment, I thought. Not into celebrating? I had a feeling that I would never figure Jamie out. But at least I had tried.

Jessi ran up to me. "I think I see the Marshmallow," she said, pointing to my mom's white van as it pulled into the parking lot. "I think you're going to have to carry me inside."

I laughed. "Come on, was that practice really too much for you?"

"Yes!" Jessi replied. "And you're lying if you say it was easy."

"Nobody said winning was going to be easy," I told her, and Jessi shook her head.

"You sound like Coach Darby."

I put on my best Coach Darby voice. "Drop and give me a thousand!" I barked, and we were both cracking up as we piled into the van.

CHAPTER FOUR

"So you're nervous about playing against Zoe?" Kara asked. Kara was my best friend back in Connecticut. She was the thing I missed most about leaving there, and we made it a point to video chat almost every day.

I was in my bedroom, talking to Kara on my laptop, and wearing my pink, white, and blue Griffons uniform.

"Not nervous, exactly," I said. "Just feeling weird. How can I want to beat the Gators when I know that Zoe wants to win as much as I do?"

Kara nodded sympathetically. "I get it. But I think you have to put it aside. I bet this happens all the time to the pros. Players are traded or move to other teams, and suddenly best friends are dueling it out on the field."

"I didn't think of that," I said. "Yeah, I just need to suck it up and do my best."

"Plus, it may give you an advantage," Kara pointed out.

"I mean, you know the strengths and weaknesses of some of the Gators already."

"I didn't think of that either," I said. "Is it possible you're getting even smarter?"

Kara grinned. "Go, Griffons!" she cheered. "Let me know how it goes tonight. I should be back from ice-skating by seven."

"Ice-skating?" I still had a hard time remembering that it was winter back in Connecticut, when it was so warm and sunny in California.

"Yeah, Matt Solomon asked me, and—"

"You're going ice-skating with Matt Solomon? Like, on a date?" I interrupted.

"No. I mean, kind of," Kara said, blushing a little. "There's a whole bunch of us going. But Matt is the one who asked me if I would go."

"I didn't know you liked him," I said. "I thought you said he was weird, after he ate those banana sandwiches every day for lunch for a whole year."

Kara shrugged. "Weird, but cute," she said, blushing again. "Hey, don't you need to get to your game?"

I looked at the time. "Oh yeah! Have fun skating."

"Have fun beating the Gators!" she called out, and then we both signed off.

Mom, Dad, and Maisie were all waiting downstairs to go to the game with me—my own personal cheering section. My dad had never missed a single one of my games, which I thought was pretty impressive. And most of the time I had all three of my biggest fans there to watch me play.

The winter league games were held at fields around the county, and the Gators game was taking place at the Rancho Verdes Middle School field. We pulled up in the Marshmallow at eleven forty-five, fifteen minutes earlier than Coach Darby had required. I saw a bunch of other Griffons on the field, which made me feel good—until I saw the mob of Gators in their purple uniforms jogging around the track. They had started their practice even earlier than we'd been planning to!

I saw Zoe's strawberry-blond head bobbing in the group of Gators. She had a look of determination on her face like I'd never seen. When Mom parked the Marshmallow, I jogged toward my teammates, trying to put that same look on my own face. The Gators were clearly in it to win, and the Griffons had to be too.

As soon as I reached the field, Coach Darby started having us do skill drills. It was earlier than noon, but I guessed that she was feeling the pressure too. After our warm-up we performed our pregame cartwheel ritual (each one of us did a cartwheel and then named someone else to do one) and then cooled down with some stretching. I gazed up into the stands.

Mom, Dad, and Maisie were all holding a long GO, DEVIN! banner. I hadn't known they were going to do that. Sometimes I thought I had the sweetest family ever.

And behind them I saw a big pink sign with GO,

GRIFFONS and a big purple sign with GO, GATORS on it, right next to each other. I had a feeling I knew who was behind those, and then I saw their faces—Emma held the Griffons sign, and Frida held the Gators sign. They had figured out a way to root for both teams.

I gave them a wave as Coach Darby called us over to the sidelines. The game was about to start.

"All right, the Gators are going to be tough to beat," she said. "So I want to see everybody give a hundred and ten percent out there. You got it?"

"Yes, Coach!" we replied.

"Let's keep that energy going!" she said. "Now let's talk about the lineup. Devin, Jamie, and Kelly, I want you on forward. My midfielders are . . ."

I didn't hear any more after that, because Coach Darby had just said she was starting me as forward! It was the first time she'd started me since my soccer slump. I felt pumped!

Jamie took the center spot as we faced off against the Gators. The ref blew his whistle, and the ball dropped. Jamie got it and kicked it sideways to Kelly, but before Kelly could receive it, one of the Gators swooped in and took control. She dribbled it down and across the field and then passed it to the Gator nearest to me—Grace from the Kicks.

An eighth grader, Grace was tall and blond, and when she moved on the field, her name said it all. I knew from playing with her that she was fast, and with her long legs she could make her way down the field in no time. I also knew that when she dribbled, she didn't keep the ball close to her. Instead she kicked it ahead and caught up to it with long strides. So I knew just what to do.

I swept in front of Grace from the side, waiting for her to pass to one of her teammates, and then bam! I was on it. I took the ball and dashed down toward the Gators goal, my heart pounding.

Then a purple streak whizzed by me. Zoe! She stole the ball right from under my feet and then zigzagged down the field with it. She was a real speed demon sometimes, and I knew her agility was tough to beat. But that didn't erase the sting.

As Zoe neared the Griffons goal line, she passed the ball to one of her teammates—and Katie, one of our defenders, intercepted it. I was glad that the Gators hadn't scored, because I'd let Zoe get the ball from me!

The rest of the first quarter was pretty much the same—the Gators got the ball, then the Griffons stole it. Then the Gators stole it back. Nobody scored. In the second quarter Coach Darby swapped out Kelly for Sasha as forward but left me and Jamie in.

Things got off to a good start. Jamie got control of the ball and passed it to me. I saw Zoe coming for me again and sent the ball to Jessi, who was playing midfield. Jessi took it toward the goal, and I stayed close by her. When one of the Gators came for Jessi, she passed the ball to me.

I was in the goal zone now, and I knew I had about five

seconds before the Gators defenders would descend on me. But I had a long, clear shot, and I took it. I sent the ball low and fast toward the goal.

The Gators goalie had to dive for it, and she missed! I had scored.

"Go, Devin!" roared Mom, Dad, Maisie, Emma, and Frida in the stands. If I had felt pumped up before, I felt superpumped now!

Then, right before the whistle blew to end the first half, the Gators scored. Grace made one of her long drives, and our defenders just couldn't catch her. She sent one sailing over the head of Courtney, our goalie.

The ref's whistle blew, and we ended the half with a score of 1–1. Coach Darby wasn't happy.

"You're letting them steal from you too much!" she reprimanded, and I felt a small pang of guilt—but only a small one, since I had been the one to score our only goal, after all. When she finished her pep talk (more like a scolding, actually), she announced the new lineup. Jessi, Jamie, and I were on the bench. This time around she put in Kelly, Sasha, and Mirabelle as forwards.

"Go, Devin!" I heard from the stands, and I looked up to see my mom, dad, and Maisie going crazy. Next to me Jamie rolled her eyes.

"They cheer for you even when you're not playing?" Jamie said. "How much do you pay them to do that?"

I just ignored her. Behind my family, I noticed that Emma and Frida had switched signs! Emma was holding the Gators sign, and Frida held the Griffons sign. They must have figured switching at the half was the fairest thing to do.

Then the whistle blew, and I kept my eyes on the game. The Griffons looked good, getting the ball down the field with a series of short passes that kept the Gators guessing. Then Mirabelle took a shot at the goal—but the Gators goalie blocked it.

Kelly, Mirabelle, and Sasha each made another goal attempt during the quarter, but they couldn't get past the goalie. The good news was, none of the Gators got past Courtney either. The third quarter ended with a score of 1–1.

"Devin, Jamie, you're back in!" Coach Darby called out, pulling out Kelly and Sasha from the forward line. Now I was back on the field with Zoe and Grace, and it was anybody's game. I felt like I had enough adrenaline running through me to rocket to the moon.

Early on I made a strong drive to the goal. I passed the ball to Jamie, and she shot it in so hard and fast that I was shocked when the goalie swatted it away. Mirabelle went for the goal again a few minutes later, but her high kick soared over the top of the net. We just couldn't score again!

And until the last few seconds of the game, it looked like the Gators couldn't score either. Until Zoe made another zigzag drive down the field, avoiding every Griffon who crossed her path. She passed the ball to one of her teammates, who found a hole in the right goal pocket and sank it in. It was 2–1.

I tried not to give up hope. There had to be a chance for the Griffons to score again! But before the next play could be set up, the ref blew his whistle. The game was over, and the Gators had won.

Both teams lined up to slap palms. I made sure to look Grace and Zoe in the eyes when I did. Zoe had such a happy look on her face that any other time I would have been thrilled for her.

But now . . . well, I wasn't feeling thrilled at all!

CHAPTER FIVE

Screeeeeeeeech!

The metal table legs made a deafening sound as we pushed four tables together at Pizza Kitchen to make room for all seventeen Griffons. We should have been eighteen, but Jamie hadn't showed up, even though I'd tried inviting her again after the game.

"Sounds like fun. We can all cry into our pepperoni," she had said before walking away.

Looking around the table now, I knew Jamie kind of had a point. Nobody looked happy at all, and nobody was really talking with one another. Even though our play-off hopes hadn't been dashed yet, this was a tough loss. Luckily, it was two thirty, and the lunch crowd was mostly gone, so if we were going to cry into our pepperoni, nobody would see us.

"Okay, so how many pizzas do we want?" I asked, just as a commotion came through the front door. A great, purple commotion of victorious Gators.

Unlike the Griffons, the Gators were talking and laughing—loudly. I caught Zoe's eye, and she flashed me an apologetic smile, but she didn't come over to talk to me or anything. She and the Gators pushed some tables together and started their victory celebration.

"Root beer for everyone!" one of the Gators yelled, and her teammates let out a cheer. I guessed that root beer must have been their victory tradition or something.

Over at our table Kelly and Sasha were whispering to each other. Then Kelly spoke up.

"Listen, it was a nice idea to come out for pizza and everything, but we should leave," she said. "I don't want to witness the Gators' victory celebration."

"It's too depressing," chimed in Sasha, and some of the other girls started to murmur in agreement.

I looked at Jessi, and she just shrugged.

"Come on. Leaving will be even more depressing," I said. "We haven't had our pizza yet. And let's not forget, if we win next week's game, we'll go to the semifinals. We might have another chance to beat the Gators."

"*If* we win next week," Tracey said.

"Of course we'll win next week!" I said. "And then we'll go on to the semifinals, and then we'll go to our championship game and crush it!"

"Yeah!" Jessi cheered, and I was so grateful that she had come around. Soon all the Griffons were cheering and pounding our fists on the table.

We calmed down long enough to figure out our pizza order, and while we waited for it, everyone was talking and laughing, just like normal. I was glad we had all decided to stay. We felt like a team—except, of course, that Jamie was missing.

"I don't understand why Jamie never comes out with us," I said.

Mirabelle was sitting next to me. "You know that I used to be friends with her, right?" she asked, and I nodded. "Well, I might know what's bugging her. She loves soccer, but her parents don't take it seriously. Her older brother plays football and basketball, and her younger sister is a ballet dancer, and Jamie's got this whole middle-child problem."

"What do you mean?" I asked.

Jessi's eyes lit up. "Wait, it's like Addison on *RTOBH*!" she said. "Her parents adore her oldest sister, who's a model, and her little sister is like a genius or something, and they ignore Addison. Jasmine said on one episode that's why Addison acts out."

"Yeah, kind of like that," agreed Mirabelle. "Jamie's parents almost never come to her soccer games. They work all the time, and when they take off work, it's to go to a football game or a dance recital. It really bothers Jamie."

"Wow, I totally get that," I said. And then it hit me—Jamie had been dropping hints all along. I just hadn't understood them.

A few games ago, when my dad had been late to my

game, Jamie had told me to "get used to it." And the other day she'd said that she didn't like celebrating, and just today she had made fun of my cheering section.

"That must be hard, to see other people's parents cheering on their kids and have nobody cheering for you," I said. "Poor Jamie!"

Jessi shook her head. "Wow, I didn't think I'd ever hear you say, 'poor Jamie,' especially after what she did to the Kicks," she said. "But I get it. That's got to be hard for her."

Then Jessi looked at me intently. "Devin, I can see those wheels turning in your brain. I know you want to fix this. But what are you going to do? You can't change Jamie's parents."

"I know," I said, but Jessi was right. The wheels in my head *were* turning. When I saw a problem, I always wanted to fix it, no matter how hard it was.

But this problem—I realized this one might be impossible to solve!

CHAPTER SIX

"Go, Maisie!" I yelled as my sister zigzagged around a defender and charged at the goal. When another defender threatened her from the left, Maisie looked around and called out a teammate's name—"Juliet!"—before passing her the ball.

Juliet received the pass and took a shot. Goal!

Bursting with pride for my little sister, I jumped up from the camp chair I had been sitting in on the side of the field, knocking it over.

"Woo-hoo!" I yelled. My mom, sitting next to me, gave a little shriek as my chair toppled onto her. Then she shook her head and laughed before getting up to cheer too.

"Soccer families stick together," Mom said as she righted my chair.

I frowned, thinking of Jamie. Her family was definitely not a soccer family, and she had no one to cheer her on.

Which was why I was cheering a little bit more for Maisie today. It made me realize how lucky I was to have such a supportive family. If I couldn't fix Jamie's problem, at least I could show my sister how much I cared.

Maisie jogged past Mom and me. "Way to go, Maisie!" I yelled. She flashed me a smile and gave a thumbs-up before putting her game face on again.

"Great communication! Way to share the ball!" my dad called out encouragingly. He was the coach of Maisie's third-grade elementary school soccer team, the Panthers. We were watching them play in the field next to Maisie's school.

Emma and Frida, his assistant coaches, were on the sidelines too. Mom and I were sitting close by. Emma was comforting a Panther named Mindy.

"I'm so embarrassed," Mindy sobbed, tears running down her cheeks. "I kicked the ball into the wrong goal!"

I felt so bad for Mindy. In her excitement after getting the ball, she had kicked it into the Panthers' goal instead of the Comets' goal. Emma knew exactly how Mindy was feeling. She had once done the same thing, scoring for the opposite team. It had happened when I'd first started playing with the Kicks. Emma had been able to laugh it off, along with the teasing that had followed. If anyone could make Mindy feel better about what had happened, it was Emma.

Emma leaned over and began talking softly to Mindy. I couldn't hear what she said, but I saw Mindy's face brighten. The tears stopped and she started to laugh. Emma continued to talk to her, and then Mindy stood up and gave Emma a high five. My dad put Mindy back into the game, and she ran onto the field, her two long braids flapping behind her and all traces of tears gone from her cheeks. Emma watched, smiling, from the sideline.

Meanwhile, Frida was passing the ball back and forth between some of the other Panthers, keeping them warmed up and ready to jump into the game.

"Imagine that inside the ball is the ancient treasure of Atlantis. You must guard the ball to keep the treasure safe," I overheard Frida say.

Frida always played soccer better when she pretended she was someone else on the field, since she needed to be acting in order to be happy. It worked for her when she was on the Kicks, and it was fun to see her use it while coaching the little girls. They totally responded to it.

"I will protect the treasure, Princess Frida," Maisie's friend Kaylin said solemnly.

Frida's eyes shone, and I knew how much she must have loved having all these kids to playact with and to call her princess! I was laughing to myself when my phone vibrated in the pocket of my shorts. I slipped it out and saw I had a text from Zoe. I hadn't heard from her since the Gators had beaten us yesterday.

Gr8 game yesterday! It was close.

I sighed. It had been close. I had really wanted to win that game and guarantee the Griffons a place in the semifinals. Thankfully, we still had one more chance.

If we win next week's game, we might have a rematch! I texted back. What I really wanted to say is, *We'll get you next time.* But part of me held back. Zoe didn't seem comfortable competing against me and Jessi. I didn't think she'd take it as I intended it, as a good-natured rivalry.

But her answer totally surprised me.

I hope not.

What? Zoe hoped the Griffons didn't win their next game? I frowned as I reread her text, thinking I must have gotten it wrong. Maybe it was the glare from the sun. I held my palm over the screen of the phone. No. That was what she'd said. I had read it right the first time.

Wait, what? You hope we don't win? I texted back, shocked. I couldn't believe Zoe would say something like that. It was totally out of character for her. Yet she had been acting kind of strange lately. . . .

No! Sorry! Zoe texted back right away. *I meant I hope we don't have a rematch. I didn't like playing against my friends.*☹

I understood where Zoe was coming from. It was weird playing against good friends. However, I couldn't help but think that if Zoe didn't want to have a rematch with the Griffons, one of our teams would have to lose along the way. I didn't want it to be the Griffons, and I was sure Zoe didn't want it to be the Gators, either. So in a way she had to be hoping we would lose our game. Knowing Zoe, I had to believe she didn't mean it in a nasty way. I knew that

I wanted the Griffons to win. If that meant the Gators losing, what could I do?

I stared at my phone as I thought about how I would reply to Zoe. I decided to just let it go. Clearly she was getting way too stressed out about the possibility of us facing off against each other on the soccer field again. Besides, I had other things to worry about, like winning our next game and securing a spot in the semifinals.

"Excuse me, Devin?" My mom's voice interrupted my thoughts. "You're here to watch your sister's soccer game, not to text."

"Yeah, sorry," I said, feeling guilty. I did want to cheer on Maisie and the Panthers. I quickly texted back to Zoe G2G before putting my phone back into my pocket.

I put the phone away at just the right moment. Mindy had the ball, and she was racing down the field toward the opposite team's goal, not her own, with a big smile on her face. As she got closer, two defenders charged her. She looked around and spotted Maisie.

"Maisie!" Mindy called. She got the ball through the defenders, and Maisie caught it. She hit the ball, low and hard, to the right corner of the net. The goalie missed it. Maisie had scored!

"Yay, Maisie!" I cried, this time using one hand to steady my chair before leaping to my feet.

"Way to go, Maisie!" my mom shouted next to me.

"Awesome teamwork, girls!" my dad yelled to his players with a huge grin on his face. Emma and Frida jumped up and down and were cheering loudly.

A few minutes later the whistle sounded. The game was over and the Panthers had won, 2–1.

"Yes!" Maisie pumped her fist into the air and then started doing this cute little victory dance. Her friends joined in, and Mindy, who had been crying her eyes out only a few minutes before, was celebrating right along with them.

I smiled, and I was clapping and cheering for the girls' victory when something struck me. Mindy had been sobbing, yet now she was dancing and laughing. Soccer had its ups and downs. Playing against your friends was just one of them. If it freaked Zoe out, she would come around. Soon we'd be laughing and joking together again. In the meantime I wouldn't let it slow me down. I had a soccer game to win!

CHAPTER SEVEN

"So, another mysterious text from Frida. It must be Monday," Jessi deadpanned as we sat down the next day at the lunch table we usually shared with Zoe, Emma, and Frida.

This morning we'd gotten a group text from Frida saying, *Meet me at our usual lunch table today. Big news!* Frida always knew how to bring the drama, whether it was in a text or onstage. It wasn't the first secretive text we had gotten from her. Usually her news was pretty big. Like, starring-in-a-movie big. I was excited to hear what she had to say.

Emma sat down next to me, with a big grin on her face. "So, do you think Frida is going to be in another movie? Or maybe Brady McCoy remembers me from the soccer fund-raiser and has fallen totally in love with me?" She got a faraway look in her eyes when she said this.

"Uh-oh!" Jessi said, alarmed. "Emma, don't go all fan girl on us again. You know it means disaster."

I nodded in agreement. "Yes, Emma, please try to stay sane. We need you!"

At Frida's last big announcement, she'd revealed she would be starring in a movie with Brady McCoy, a teen pop star who was Emma's favorite singer in the world. Emma had all his posters up in her room, knew the lyrics to every one of his songs, and even belonged to his fan club, the Real McCoys. When she'd heard Frida would be starring in a movie with Brady, she had completely wigged out. It was what had caused her to blow her winter league soccer tryout.

Emma shook her head like she was trying to shake the image of Brady McCoy from her mind. She let out a big sigh. "Since I'm not even allowed to date yet, it would be hard for me to get together with Brady McCoy. But maybe I could convince my mom."

"Brady McCoy?" Zoe asked as she took the empty seat next to Emma. "I heard he was dating that singer Star Evans."

"You guys are such downers," Emma complained. "Can't I have a daydream without you all ruining it?"

"Hi, Zoe!" Jessi said cheerfully. "What a game on Saturday, huh? We almost had you."

"Yeah, great game." Zoe shifted in her chair, looking uncomfortable. "Hey, Devin," she said, and looked at me. "I'm sorry about that text. I hope you didn't misunderstand me."

"What text?" Emma asked loudly and innocently,

having no idea what we were talking about.

"Oh, it's nothing," I said, waving my hand in the air. "It's no big deal, Zoe. I promise."

"The Panthers won!" Emma jumped into the conversation with enthusiasm, thankfully forgetting about the text. "They did such a good job. I was so proud of them."

"You're a great coach, Emma. A total natural," I told her. Emma blushed a little bit. "Aw, well, so is Frida."

"Speaking of Frida, where is she? Her fan club is here and waiting," Jessi joked as she took a bite out of her sandwich.

For some reason the phrase "fan club" made me think of Jamie and how she didn't have one. I frowned.

Noticing my expression change, Emma asked, "What's wrong, Devin?"

"Saturday after the game the Griffons all went out for pizza. Jamie's the only one who didn't come—" I started to explain, but got cut off.

"Good! Lucky you," Emma said. I understood why Emma, who was usually a total sweetie, would say something like that. Jamie had gotten all of the Kicks really upset when she had tried to sabotage our team.

"That's what I would have thought a couple of weeks ago, but now I'm not so sure. Jamie is the outsider on the team, and Mirabelle told me some stuff that made me feel bad for Jamie," I said.

"Like she felt bad when she was writing 'Loser' on your jersey, Devin?" Zoe asked, reminding me of just one of the many nasty tricks Jamie had pulled.

"I know, I know," I said. Zoe had a point. "Jamie did a lot of mean things. But Mirabelle was saying how her parents work all the time and never go to her games, yet they take time off to go to her brother's football games and her sister's dance recitals. Her parents aren't really into soccer. I'm not sure if they've even been to one of her games!" I couldn't keep the shock out of my voice as I said that. It was hard to imagine my parents not being excited about my games. It made me sad to even think about it.

"That is terrible," Emma, who always looked for the best in everyone, said. "But be careful around Jamie, Devin. You can't trust her."

"Jessi has a good theory on Jamie, about Addison on *RTOBH*," I said, looking to Jessi for support. But before I could get that conversation going, Frida appeared.

"I'm sorry. Am I late?" Frida asked as she placed a hand dramatically on her forehead.

"Knock it off, Frida, and tell us your news!" said Jessi, direct as always.

"Well." Frida brushed her long, auburn curls off her shoulder as she stood at the head of the table, not taking a seat. She was making this announcement standing up and as the center of attention. *So* Frida. "I'm here to tell you that *Mall Mania* has a release date. It will air in one month on the BubblePop cable network."

"We'll finally get to see it! Cool!" Emma said, her eyes shining with enthusiasm.

"Yes, and that's not all," Frida said, her voice full of

excitement. "There's going to be a big premiere in Los Angeles the night before the movie airs on television. I'm going to get to walk the red carpet!"

"Wow!" Zoe said, awestruck. "The red carpet! What are you going to wear?"

"That's where I'll need all of you. Especially you, Zoe. I need help picking out the perfect dress," Frida said.

"Of course!" Zoe answered as she clapped her hands together. "It'll be so much fun."

"I wish you could all be there at the red carpet premiere with me." Frida made a frowny face. "But the television premiere will be the next night, and I'll throw a party for that at my house. We can watch it together."

"Now, this is something right out of *RTOBH*," Jessi said. "How cool! Can Cody and Steven come?"

"Well, I haven't worked out the guest list yet, but I'm sure we can squeeze them in," she joked.

I was excited about Frida's news too. I actually knew someone who was going to walk on the red carpet! And her party sounded like fun. Yet I had to do a quick mental calendar check. "What day of the week is the party at your house?" I asked.

"Saturday night, in four weeks, and you all just have to be there, or I will cancel this party," Frida threatened dramatically.

Four weeks. The regular season games would be over this weekend. I did the math for the semifinals game and then the championship game.

"Oh good," I said before I could stop myself. "That

would be the week after the winter league championship game, so there's no conflict."

"No conflict? This could be a disaster! What if it's Griffons versus Gators?" Frida asked, her voice rising. "One of you would be the winners and one would be the losers. That could mean serious conflict at my party!" The way she said it, she almost sounded a little hopeful. Like she wouldn't mind some conflict at her party.

The vibe at our table got slightly uncomfortable. Zoe shifted in her seat, not making eye contact with anyone. Emma looked upset. I felt a little annoyed with Frida for getting everyone worried about nothing.

Jessi and I exchanged glances. "Relax, Frida. It's just a game," Jessi said, trying to talk her down. "We're friends. There wouldn't be any fighting."

I looked at Zoe's face as Jessi said that, and she looked a little pale. "We don't even know who will be in the championships yet," she said softly.

"Yeah, so let's not worry about it," Jessi added.

Emma forced a smile. "Well, if it is Griffons versus Gators, Frida's party might be just what we'd all need to take our minds off the outcome!"

"Yes, or it could be where all the tension boils over!" Frida said, and I could tell she was imagining a crazy scene in her mind, with Zoe and me pulling each other's hair out or something.

I had to put a stop to this. It was getting ridiculous.

"We're all worrying about something that may not

happen," I said, trying to keep my voice calm. "First of all, the Griffons haven't made it to the semifinals. And if we do, there's no predicting if we'll make it to the championships, or if the Gators will either." I was kind of lying when I said this last part. I had every intention of making it to the championship game. But I didn't want to give Frida—or Zoe—any more of a reason to worry at the moment. I knew we had to beat two other teams. And if we lost the game this Saturday, we wouldn't even be playing in the semifinals. But I was going to do everything I could to make sure that didn't happen.

"All right, Devin. If you say so, I won't worry about it," Frida said as she sat down and pulled a notebook out of her backpack. "I've got tons of party planning to do, anyway. Where should we begin?"

The tension eased as everyone started sharing ideas. As they all chatted, I thought back to the last game we'd had with the Gators. It had been tough. The other teams in the winter league were just as good as the Gators too. I had been feeling positive we could beat the Giraffes in our last regular season game this Saturday and ensure our spot in the semifinals. Now I wasn't so sure. *If it means being in the championship game*, I thought, *I'd rather have drama at Frida's party than be on a losing team that doesn't even make it to the semifinals!*

CHAPTER EIGHT

"Are you crazy?" Jessi asked me in disbelief. "My legs feel like spaghetti right now. Devin, you are some kind of machine!"

That was her reaction after practice the next day when I told her I was going for a run. It had been another practice where Coach Darby had pushed us to the limit.

"We've got to win our game against the Giraffes," I reminded her. "So I'm amping up my training. You're welcome to join me."

Jessi shook her head, her long braids swinging. "I'm going to go home, take a shower, eat dinner, and do some homework. Then I'll reward myself with some *Real Teenagers*. Taylor has a plan to get even with Addison for ruining her birthday party!"

When I got home, as I jogged through our neighborhood, I thought of Jessi taking a refreshing shower and watching television. Maybe she had the right idea. Crashing on the couch with some TV was tempting. My legs ached as I pumped them. But I gritted my teeth and kept going. I had to be tougher and faster than the Giraffes on Saturday, so this was what I needed to do.

When I turned a corner ten blocks away from my house, I noticed a familiar strawberry-blond head bobbing up and down ahead of me. It was Zoe! Looked like I wasn't the only one who was training extra hard.

"Hey, Zoe!" I called out, excited to see her. It would be nice to have someone to run with. It might even help me take my mind off my legs, which were begging me to stop.

I saw Zoe's head turn slightly at the sound of my voice, but instead of stopping or turning around, she began to run faster. I could have sworn she saw me out of the corner of her eye.

"Zoe, wait up!" I yelled again, in case she truly hadn't seen or heard me. I sped up to catch her, but she went down another street. By the time I caught up to the corner where she had turned, Zoe had disappeared from sight.

Did Zoe see me and ignore me on purpose? I thought. I knew Zoe was uncomfortable competing against me, but did that mean we couldn't even hang out anymore? Things were really getting so strange between us. Yet I couldn't let it bother me. I had a game to win on Saturday!

On Saturday morning I woke up early, ready to get onto the soccer field and fight my way into the semifinals.

As I ate my breakfast of oatmeal, a banana, and whole wheat toast, I looked out the window. The sky was dark and cloudy. We'd been experiencing a drought in California, and I knew we desperately needed rain. But why did it have to be today?

My dad noticed my concern. "You can still play in the rain, Devin," he said. "In fact, it might even give you an advantage. You've played in the rain a lot more in Connecticut than these California girls have."

"Good point, Dad," I said. He always knew how to look on the bright side.

Then he handed me a glass of orange juice, and I thought of Zoe. When I'd been in my soccer slump, she had helped me out of it. One of her tips was to drink orange juice before a game to help keep me calm. I felt kind of sad thinking about her. After my run on Tuesday, I hadn't gotten a chance to talk to her about what had happened. She'd been eating lunch all week with the Gators. The whole situation was awkward. I couldn't dwell on it now. I had to get my head in the game and keep it there.

I went upstairs to put on my uniform. The pink, white, and blue went perfectly with the pink headband I wore at every game. My headband was a tradition I'd brought with me from Connecticut to California. I believed it brought me luck on the field. I was ready to do this!

I felt the butterflies doing the cha-cha in my stomach as Dad pulled into the Pinewood Recreation Center parking lot. If we lost this game, the season would be over for the Griffons.

As we got out of the Marshmallow, I got hugs from my family. They were all wearing Griffons pink, even my dad, who had bought a pink polo shirt just to wear to our games.

"Good luck, Devin!" Maisie said as she gave me a big hug. I couldn't help but think of Jamie. I was so lucky to have my family's support and encouragement.

"Bye!" I said to them as I raced toward the field. I saw that some of the other Griffons were already there, warming up.

"Devin, don't forget to hydrate!" Mom reminded me. She was always telling me to drink more water. I held my water bottle up so she could see it.

"Got it, Mom!" I said.

I tossed my stuff onto the sidelines and caught up with the rest of my team, who were eyeing the sky nervously as they stretched and kicked the ball around.

"I thought I heard thunder," Jessi said as she walked toward me. "They might cancel the game!"

I groaned. "Oh no, I hope not! I'm all pumped up for this game. If it's rescheduled, I'll have to get pumped up all over again."

"They won't let us play if there's a lightning threat," Tracey chimed in nervously. "It's really dangerous, you know."

I looked up. Black clouds were chasing one another

across the sky. It definitely looked like it was going to do *something*.

Coach Darby clapped her hands.

"All right, girls, don't let a little bad weather get to you!" she said. "If there's a game delay, we'll know soon. Until then let's focus on what we want to accomplish today. You've been giving me your all at practices. I've been impressed with what I've been seeing on the field. You are ready to claim your place in the semifinals. You've earned it!"

It was the most encouraging speech she'd ever given us. It made me feel proud to be a Griffon. Then . . . *Boom!* Thunder exploded overhead. Everyone jumped, even Coach Darby. I'd thought that nothing scared her!

"That sounded close," she said as the ref walked over to her.

"Clear the field," he told her. "We're clearing the stands, too. We've got a lightning delay."

Ugh! My legs twitched. They wanted to be on the soccer field, scoring. But instead they had to march inside to the locker room. I waved to my pink-clad family as they moved with the crowd into the rec center.

"Don't lose focus," Coach Darby reminded us. "Once it's clear, we'll be back on the field."

As our team nervously milled around inside the locker room, the tension became unbearable.

"Hey! There's not enough room to do our cartwheels in here, but let's toss the soccer ball around," I said, figuring it might give us something to focus on. I grabbed a soccer ball out of one of the lockers. "We'll do it the same way we do the cartwheels. Call someone's name before throwing them the ball."

Everyone eagerly gathered around in a circle, except for Jamie, who was sitting on a bench and didn't get up.

"Jamie?" I asked, but she just rolled her eyes at me and shook her head.

I shrugged. I wouldn't let her bring us down.

"Courtney!" I said as I tossed the ball to our goalie. We all threw the ball back and forth and began joking as we did. We even began to make up silly nicknames for one another as we threw the ball.

"Sasha Fierce!"

"Awesome Amanda!"

"Devin the Destroyer!" (I really liked that one.)

Then the ref came in and told us we could get back onto the field. The lightning had moved away, and the game could begin.

Outside, it was still cloudy, but there were breaks in the clouds where you could see the sun. I took that as a good sign.

The Giraffes won the toss and chose to receive first, but Jessi quickly got possession of the ball. As she dribbled down the field, three Giraffes charged her. I saw the panic on her face.

"Jessi! I'm open!" I called, which brought a Giraffe running over to try to intercept the pass Jessi sent my way.

But all my running had paid off. I was simply faster than the defender. I got to the ball first and moved it closer to the goal before taking a shot. The ball bounced off the crossbar and right back at me. I jumped up into the air to meet the ball and headed it into the goal. It all happened so fast that the goalie didn't see it coming.

"Devin!" Jessi came over and high-fived me, as did a bunch of my other teammates. "That was spectacular!"

Even Jamie gave me a grudging nod. "Good job," she said gruffly.

Scoring only a minute into the game set the tone. The Giraffes, already thrown off by the lightning delay just as we had been, lost even more confidence after our goal. Meanwhile, it gave the Griffons a ton of confidence, and we were the clear aggressors for the rest of the game.

At the half it was 3–0, Griffons. After the break it was clear the Giraffes had gotten some of their self-assurance back. A few seconds in, one of their midfielders intercepted the ball and dribbled it down, passing it to one of the forwards. She shot it right into the goal.

The Giraffes got possession of the ball a few more times, but our defense kept getting the ball back and eliminating any scoring threats. We were on fire!

At the end of the game, it was 3–1 in favor of the Griffons.

"We're going to the semifinals!" Jessi cheered, and we hugged each other, jumping up and down.

CHAPTER Nine

"Okay, so we need to get started right away. We've got a lot to go over," Frida said on Monday at lunch as Jessi, Emma, and I sat down. "Did everyone bring food, like I asked, so we don't waste time waiting in line?"

"I always bring my lunch," I said, unwrapping my hummus-and-sprouts pita wrap. "My mom says that cafeteria lunches are a nutritional joke."

"Maybe, but tater tots are delicious," Emma said with a longing look at the menu board. "I love tater tot day!"

Jessi looked at Emma's fancy cloth lunch bag. "So, what did your mom pack you?"

Emma looked inside. "Ham and brie on a baguette with honey mustard; fruit salad; and carrot sticks with tarragon dip."

Jessi's eyes got wide. "And you're wishing for tater tots? Seriously? Tell you what, you can trade it all for my PB&J and squeezable yogurt."

Emma shook her head. "No way. I may have to give up tater tots, but I'm not giving up my brie."

"Can we focus, please?" Frida asked. "This is exactly the kind of thing I wanted to avoid. I've got a lot of planning to do for this movie premiere and my party, and I need your help."

She pulled a notebook and a stack of magazines from her backpack. "I need a menu, and a red carpet dress, and a dress for my party, and—" She stopped. "Hey, where's Zoe?"

I scanned the cafeteria. Zoe and some of the Gators were sitting at a table in the corner.

"She's over there," I said with a nod.

"But she *must* have gotten my text," Frida said. "This is important. She's the only one of you guys with any real fashion sense!"

"Hey!" Emma protested, and Jessi and I just shook our heads.

"Well, it's true and you know it," Frida said. "No offense or anything, but Zoe just really has her eye on all the trends. And my mom won't let me get a stylist for the red carpet, so I need Zoe's help."

"Well, why don't you just ask her to come over here?" I asked. That would have been the simple, sensible thing to do, right? But Frida wasn't simple, and when she was riled up about something, she was usually not too sensible.

"I know she got my text," Frida said, sounding annoyed. "But I guess whatever's happening with the Gators is more important than my movie premiere."

I understood why Frida was upset, but I thought I knew where Zoe was coming from too.

"Try to think of it from her point of view," I said. "The winter league championships are kind of like the movie premiere of soccer, you know? So that's where she's focusing all her energy."

"That's true!" Emma said, sticking up for Zoe. "That's all she talks about lately!"

"Well, she could have texted me and told me," Frida said defensively.

"Frida's right," said Jessi. "I mean, Zoe's kind of been ignoring us lately."

I knew Jessi had a point. "I still think you should talk to her," I told Frida.

Frida glanced over at the Gators table. "No, that's fine. I can go over the red carpet dress with her some other time. You guys can help me with the menu for the party at my house. I wanted to do something fancy, but the movie is set in a mall. And caviar and malls don't seem to go together."

"Ooh, I know!" said Emma, bouncing in her seat. "You should serve the kinds of food you get at the mall. Like hot pretzels and corn dogs and stuff like that."

Frida's eyes brightened. "Hey, that's not a bad idea! Plus my mom said there was no way she would serve caviar anyway. But she won't say no to corn dogs."

"Menu accomplished," said Emma. "Can we eat now?"

"Yes, but we need to keep brainstorming," Frida said.

"Like some mall-themed beverages and a mall-themed dessert. And what color should I do the plates and cups and decorations?"

"Isn't there a logo for the movie?" I asked. I had remembered seeing it on a T-shirt Frida had worn.

Frida showed me a picture on her phone of the words "Mall Mania" with zigzag lines and hearts around them. The logo was pink on an orange background.

"How about pink and orange?" I suggested.

"I love that combination," Jessi said.

Frida nodded. "I could get pink and orange flowers, and pink and orange balloons . . . but then what color dress would I wear? I'd have to pick something that won't clash."

She glanced over at Zoe again, and I got ready for her to start complaining. Luckily, Cody and Steven walked up just then.

"Good job getting into the semifinals," Cody said.

"Yeah, so do you guys play the Gators next?" Steven asked.

"Not yet," I replied. "We'll face the Grizzlies in the semifinals next, and the Gators will face the Gazelles. Then the winner from each of those games will play each other for the championship."

"Oh, I get it!" Emma piped up.

I could see Emma picturing the whole slate in her head. "So, if the Griffons win your game on Saturday, and the Gators win their game on Saturday, you'll both be playing each other for the winter league championship?"

"That's right," Jessi said.

"Well, good luck," Steven said, and the boys walked off. Emma and Frida exchanged glances.

"I hope you're not worried about who to root for again," I said. "Like I said before, it doesn't matter."

"Well, I guess we'll just wait and see what happens!" Emma said cheerfully. Then she turned to Frida. "You know what would be cool at your house? A pink-and-orange carpet instead of a red carpet! You could put it in the hallway for when everyone walks in."

Frida and Emma started talking about party decorations, and I glanced over at Zoe's table. I had to give it to Zoe, she was superfocused on winning that championship.

But so was I.

CHAPTER TEN

Win . . . win . . . win . . ., I repeated over and over as I jogged around the track, my ponytail bouncing against my neck in time with the chant. *Win . . . win . . . win . . .*

It was Thursday afternoon, and Coach Darby was putting us through another grueling practice to prepare for our semifinal game coming up on Saturday. We would be playing the Grizzlies. We had beaten them the last time we'd played them—but no thanks to me.

The last Grizzlies game had come right after I had been shaken up by my first California earthquake. Coach Darby had started me in the game, and I'd gone offsides in the first few minutes! Right after that I had missed an easy pass that had been intercepted by one of the Grizzlies, and they'd gone on to score! I'd lost focus after that, and I'd missed another easy pass—and that was when Coach Darby had benched me and put Jamie in my place.

As I jogged another lap now, I practiced one of the techniques Zoe had taught me. I pictured the Grizzlies game in my head. This time when the pass rolled to me, I was right on it. I stopped the ball with my foot and then charged down the field, breezing by every defender who tried to stop me. The goalie's eyes were glued to me, but I wasn't afraid. I kicked the ball hard and to the right of her, and she dove for it . . . and missed!

"Score!" I cheered out loud, because the whole scene in my head seemed so real. Jessi, who was jogging next to me, gave me a look.

"Let me guess," she said. "There's a soccer game going on in your head right now."

"Something like that," I told her.

She grinned and shook her head. "You are so obsessed! Come on. Race you to the finish."

Then she tore off ahead of me, and I raced to catch up. We crossed the finish line at the same time and then high-fived.

One by one the rest of the Griffons crossed the line behind us. A few girls immediately flopped onto the grass outside the track. Coach Darby had really worked us hard again.

"Good effort today, girls!" Coach Darby said. "I'm calling for another practice tomorrow, same time."

There were a few groans, but Coach Darby silenced them with a steely glare.

I raised my hand. "Coach, we had started to plan

another team building activity for tomorrow, but we can always do it after practice."

"Like another pizza party?" Jamie asked, rolling her eyes.

"No, I was actually thinking maybe we could go to the ice-skating rink," I said.

"We're not risking any broken ankles!" Coach Darby snapped. "But if you girls want to do something that will build teamwork, I've got a few thoughts. Leave it to me."

I was a little surprised. We had never included Coach on our team building outings before, but of course, she was part of the team too. I was dying to ask what she had in mind, but I knew better.

"See you at practice tomorrow," she said. "I'll e-mail your parents about the team building once I've got the details worked out."

"What do you think she has in mind?" I asked Jessi as we walked toward the parking lot.

"I don't know. What would Coach Darby think is fun? Pounding bricks with a sledgehammer?" Jessi wondered.

I laughed. "Oh gosh, now I'm scared! What if it's something awful?"

I was so anxious to find out what Coach Darby had planned that I bugged my mom and dad all night to see if they had received an e-mail from her. Finally, at eight fifteen, Mom came into my room when I was doing homework.

"Okay, I got the e-mail from Coach Darby," Mom said.

I practically jumped out of my chair. "What does it say?"

"Practice is from three to four thirty," Mom replied. "Then she's giving you a dinner break and asking everyone to report to 123 Lavender Drive in Kentville at five forty-five. Then we're supposed to pick you up at seven."

"123 Lavender Drive?" I asked. "Is that where Coach lives? Does she want us to paint her house or something?"

Mom shrugged. "I guess you'll find out tomorrow."

I looked out the car window as Jessi's mom pulled up to 123 Lavender Drive at 5:43 p.m. The long, L-shaped building was set back from the road, and pink and purple flowers grew along the brick walkway leading to the front door. The sign over the door read, WELCOME TO LAVENDER HILLS.

"I still don't get what we're doing," I said as Jessi and I walked up to the door.

"Well, we're about to find out," said Jessi.

We rang the doorbell. Then there was a buzzing sound, and a voice said, "Come in." We pushed open the door and found ourselves in a lobby with gleaming white floors. Tracey, Katie, Kristin, and Kelly were standing in front of a desk.

"What's going on?" I asked them.

"Coach Darby said to wait here until everyone gets here," Kristin said with a shrug.

I looked around and pretty quickly figured out where we were, at least. I could see an open doorway with a sign that read COMMUNITY ROOM over the top, and when I peeked inside, I saw a bunch of elderly people sitting at tables and talking. Coach Darby was talking to a white-haired woman in a wheelchair. So Lavender Hills was some kind of retirement home or nursing home. But what were we doing here?

The rest of the Griffons started pouring through the front door. Nobody wanted to be late for Coach Darby's five forty-five start time. I was surprised to see Jamie there, and she noticed the look on my face.

"Yeah, well, Coach Darby asked us to come," she explained, and I knew that meant, "I wouldn't have come if *you* had asked me."

Then Coach Darby marched into the lobby. "Thanks for coming, ladies!" she said. "Tonight is game night here at Lavender Hills. These folks could use some fresh competition. Follow me."

Jessi and I exchanged glances, surprised.

"A game night with old people?" Jessi whispered. "That seems very un-Darby-like."

The other girls were whispering too, and I knew we were all wondering why Coach Darby had chosen this for our activity.

Coach led us into the community room and started barking orders just like she did when we were on the field.

"Sasha, Zarine, Amanda, you're playing dominoes with Mr. Santos and Mrs. Bellworth," she said, pointing to two of the residents. "Jamie, Devin, Jessi, you're playing Scrabble with Mrs. Darby. Kelly, Lauren . . ."

Coach Darby kept calling out assignments as Jamie, Jessi, and I headed toward the white-haired woman in the wheelchair whom Coach Darby had pointed to. As soon as we got there, Jessi blurted out the question rolling around in my mind.

"Hi, Mrs. Darby! Are you Coach Darby's mom?" Jessi asked, taking a seat next to her.

The woman grinned. "I sure am. Don't know why she didn't tell you. Barb's a good girl, but she never did learn her manners correctly," she said.

I had to stop myself from laughing out loud. No manners! Yup, that sounded like Coach Darby. But that wasn't the best thing Mrs. Darby had said.

Jamie caught on right away. "Wait a minute. Her name is Barb? Short for Barbara? Or Barbie?"

"She always hated being called Barbie," Mrs. Darby said. "You know, Barbie Darby. Don't know why I didn't think of that when I named her. She never let me live that down."

Jamie looked at me and smiled. Barbie Darby! This was hilarious.

Mrs. Darby started setting up the Scrabble board and passing out letter tiles. Her hair was white from age, not from hair dye, but it was basically the same color as her daughter's. And they both had the same piercing blue eyes.

"I hope you girls have good vocabularies," she said. "I can't find anyone around here who can put together anything bigger than a six-letter word. It's just no fun."

"I got a ninety-five on my last vocabulary test," Jessi offered.

Mrs. Darby nodded. "Then you won't disappoint me. Now, everyone pick a letter so we can see who goes first."

Jamie ended up with the first turn, and she made the word "festive" right off the bat. "Seven letters. There you go," she said proudly.

Mrs. Darby nodded. "Nicely done. Barb said she had a good group of girls on this team."

We had a good time playing the game, but the most fun was that Jamie and Jessi kept asking Mrs. Darby questions about Coach Darby. Like, what food did she refuse to eat when she was a kid? (Broccoli.) And did she sleep with any stuffed animals? (Mr. Stompers, an elephant.) Mrs. Darby was telling us a funny story about how Coach Darby had gotten lost on the way home from school one day, when Jamie's cell phone rang.

"It's my dad," she said apologetically, and answered it. "Yeah. But it's not seven yet."

Then she sighed. "I have to go now. We have to get my sister from dance practice," she said. "Sorry."

Mrs. Darby looked at the score sheet. "That's a shame, dear. You're winning."

Jamie didn't reply; she just nodded good-bye and then hurried out of the room. I felt really bad for her, watching her go.

We'd been having fun. And getting along. Which was exactly what a team building exercise was supposed to do. And then Jamie had had to leave.

Mrs. Darby was right. That was a real shame!

CHAPTER ELEVEN

"Mirabelle!"

"Jamie!"

"Sasha!"

"Kelly!"

It was a sunny Saturday morning on the Rancho Verdes Middle School field, and the Griffons were performing their pregame cartwheel ritual. I had started it off, and as my teammates took their turns, I gazed at the scene.

There were no bleachers on the Rancho Verdes field, so spectators had to bring their own chairs and blankets, and some had even brought umbrellas. The brown-and-white-wearing Grizzlies fans had gathered on one side of the field, and the pink, blue, and white Griffons fans were on the other side.

I looked through the crowd and saw Mom, Dad, and Maisie, and Jessi's parents. Emma and Frida were there, and I knew that they planned to leave at halftime to go see the end of Zoe's game. I wondered if either of Jamie's parents had showed up, but I realized I didn't even know what they looked like.

Coach Darby blew her whistle. "Okay, girls, gather round!"

Jamie sidled up to me as we huddled together. "I wonder what kind of speech Barbie Darby's going to give us," she whispered, and I tried not to laugh. "Demolition Darby" was a great nickname for our coach, but I would never get tired of saying "Barbie Darby."

"The Grizzlies have been defeated only once before," Coach Darby began. "And that was by us! But don't think they're going to go down without a fight. I want to see a lot of energy out there. Look for passing opportunities, and don't be afraid to score. Got it?"

"Yes, Coach!" we yelled, and then we all clapped our hands. It was game time.

Coach Darby's faith in me had returned, and she put me in as forward along with Jessi and Jamie. It was exactly where I wanted to be. Everyone on the Griffons had one goal: to win. But I had a second one: to redeem myself. My last game against the Grizzlies had been a personal disaster. I'd started off by making a goal that didn't count because I was offsides, and after that I had kept missing easy passes. Our team had won the game, but I wanted to do better this time.

The first quarter of this game started off with a bang,

with Jamie getting possession and passing it to Mirabelle, who passed it to Jessi, who passed it to Kelly, who passed it to me. I passed it back to Jamie, who lobbed it at the goal, but the Grizzlies goalie made a spectacular save, jumping up like she had springs in her cleats, and catching the ball.

The Grizzlies made a drive to our goal, but one of our defenders, Katie, intercepted it before they could attempt to score. That started another passing chain down the field. Katie to Kelly, Kelly to Mirabelle, Mirabelle to Jessi.

Jessi took the ball down to the goal line, and I traveled with her in case she needed to pass. When she was close enough, she kicked it high toward the goal, but I could see that it was veering too sharply to the right. That was when I took a cue from the Grizzlies goalie and jumped up as high as I could.

I stopped the ball with my chest. It bounced at my feet, and I quickly kicked it.

Wham! It flew into the goal, past the shocked goalie.

Redemption!

Jessi and I high-fived.

"Spectacular!" Coach Darby called out, and I beamed with pride as I jogged back down the field. I'd redeemed myself.

Now I just had to keep the momentum going.

Despite the fact that Jamie and I had been getting along, she was supercompetitive with me on the field. And that was fine, as long as she didn't elbow me or hog the ball. Determined not to be outdone, Jamie made a long drive down the field, twisting and turning to avoid the Grizzlies defenders. When she got close to the goal, she kicked the ball so low and fast that it was a white blur as it skidded across the grass, past the goalie, and into the net.

At the end of the first quarter, the score was Griffons 2, Grizzlies 0. But the Grizzlies came back in the second quarter to score, so we started the half with Griffons up, 2–1.

At the halftime break I was chugging water when Emma and Frida walked up.

"Hey, Devin, look who we found!" Emma said.

I looked up to see a woman wearing a Kangaroos T-shirt, her brown hair tied back in a messy ponytail.

"Coach Flores!" I cried, and I tackled her with a hug. "Oh, sorry. Sweaty."

Coach Flores was the coach of the Kicks during the regular season. She was the kindest, nicest coach I'd ever had, and I missed her now that the Kicks season was over. I still got to see her in school, but it just wasn't the same.

Jessi ran up as soon as she saw Coach Flores and gave her a hug too.

"You guys are looking great out there," Coach Flores said. "When Emma and Frida told me that your team and Zoe's team were both in the semifinals, I knew I had to come see you."

"She's our ride," Emma explained. "We're going to Zoe's game next."

"And she's coming to my premiere party," Frida announced.

"Of course I am! How often do I get to celebrate with a real-life movie star?" Coach Flores said, and Frida beamed at the remark.

"I'm so glad you came," I told Coach Flores. "That means a lot."

"And I'll be at the finals game next week," Coach Flores said. "I hope I'll see both of your teams there!"

Coach Flores must have noticed the worried look that crossed my face when she said that. I know I said it before, but Coach Flores was way different from Coach Darby. She was kind and understanding and always seemed to know how we were feeling.

"Just remember, Devin, that when you boil it all down, soccer is just a game. And friendship is stronger than any game," she said.

I nodded. "Thanks for saying that."

She turned to Emma and Frida. "We'd better get going." We said our good-byes, and then it was time for the second half.

"The Grizzlies are on our heels!" Coach Darby warned. "Jamie, that was a great drive in the first quarter, but you were lucky. I want you girls to pass, pass, pass."

Coach kept me, Jessi, and Jamie in as forwards. I had so much energy inside me as we ran back onto the field for the second half, I thought I might explode.

For a second I had a Frida moment.

I am a warrior beast! No Grizzly shall stand in my way! I thought, eyeing the opposition as we took our places on the field.

Bam! We were on fire. Jessi to Jamie. Jamie to me. Me to Kelly. Kelly to Jamie. Jamie to Jessi . . . and then Jessi took it right up to the goal and slammed it in.

3–1! Just seconds into the second half, and we had bolstered our lead. I knew the rest of my teammates were channeling the same energy that I was. I could feel it.

The rest of the game was a blur. Jamie scored again right before the end of the third quarter. The Grizzlies came back with another goal, bringing the score to 4–2. Then in the fourth quarter I got into a flow with Mirabelle as we passed the ball back and forth to each other, sending the Grizzlies defense into a scramble. Then Mirabelle sent the ball flying over the goalie's head.

Griffons 5, Grizzlies 2. Then the final whistle blew, and all of the Griffons went wild. We jumped up and down and screamed and hugged one another.

"We're going to the finals!" Kelly screamed.

In anticipation of the coming game, Jessi launched us into our team cheer.

"I believe!" she shouted.

"I believe!" we repeated.

"I believe that we . . . ," Jessi continued.

"I believe that we . . . ," we echoed.

"I believe that we can win . . . ," Jessi cried.

"I believe that we can win . . ."

"I believe that we can win THE FINALS!" Jessie yelled, and we all started chanting with her.

"I believe that we can win the finals! I believe that we can win the finals!"

When we all said it together like that, our voices ringing across the field, I felt in my bones that we would!

CHAPTER TWELVE

"We've got to celebrate!" Jessi said after we had finished shaking hands with the Grizzlies, who all looked really sad. I couldn't blame them. Their season was over. The Griffons were the ones going to the championships. For us that was a reason to party!

"I'm starving," I said as my stomach growled. I had burned off the yogurt fruit smoothie I'd had for breakfast, and then some!

Kristin overheard me. "Seriously, can we do something else besides pizza?" she asked.

"How about the Burrito Bowl?" Jessi suggested, practically drooling. "I could devour a Fat Sam's Superspicy Stuffed Burrito right now!"

All the burritos at the Burrito Bowl had funny names. My favorite was the Cluck-cluck-tacular Chicken Burrito Bowl. Although, sometimes I felt a little silly ordering it.

"Hey, who wants to celebrate at the Burrito Bowl?" I yelled to the rest of my teammates, who all still had smiles plastered onto their faces. Of course they were smiling. I was too. We had a shot at being the winter league champions!

Everyone liked the idea of the Burrito Bowl, and they went to talk to their families to coordinate rides to the restaurant. As I was speaking with my mom, I noticed Jamie walking to the parking lot, alone, as usual.

"I'll be right back," I told Mom as I darted after Jamie.

Jamie had been a big part of our team's win today, and she deserved to be with us as we celebrated. Although I pretty much expected a snarky response in return to the invitation, I was going to give it a try anyway.

"Hey, Jamie," I said as I caught up to her. "We're going to the Burrito Bowl to celebrate. You should be there. Want to come?"

I held my breath, waiting for a sarcastic comment, but instead Jamie looked at the ground and shrugged.

"I would if I had a ride." She sounded embarrassed. "But I don't. My brother has practice, so I've got to leave with my dad now." She gestured to a jeep parked in the lot. I saw an older man sitting in it, talking on his cell phone. I guessed that was Jamie's father.

"Don't go anywhere," I told her. "In fact, come with me."

I grabbed her arm and pulled her back to my mother. "But, Devin, my dad is waiting," Jamie protested.

"This will take only a second," I insisted. I spotted my

dad and Maisie talking with Jessi and her mom while my mother was packing up the camp chairs.

"Hey, Mom," I said. "Jamie needs a ride to the Burrito Bowl. Can we give her one? Please?" The words came out in a rush.

Jamie pulled her arm away from me. "It's okay, Devin," she said, rolling her eyes.

"Of course we can give Jamie a ride," my mom answered, ignoring Jamie's eye roll. "Do you need a ride home too?"

Jamie nodded. "I live in Riverdale," she said.

"That's only one town over," Mom said. "No problem, Jamie. You're welcome to ride with us."

"I don't want to be a bother," Jamie protested. Her cheeks got a little red.

"Like I said, no problem!" Mom answered cheerfully. "So it's settled then?" She smiled at Jamie. I couldn't believe it, but Jamie actually smiled back.

"Thanks, Mrs. Burke. I'm just going to go tell my dad," Jamie said as she raced off to the parking lot.

Before I knew it, my mom was wrapping her arms around me, giving me a big hug. "You know, sweetie, I am so proud of you as a soccer player. But I'm also so proud of the person you are too."

Mom knew everything that Jamie had put me and the Kicks through during the regular season, so she understood how reaching out to Jamie now was, well, complex, to say the least.

"Aw, Mom," I said. Now it was my turn to feel

embarrassed, with Mom getting all mushy with me on the soccer field. But it felt really nice to hear her say that.

Jamie came running back and said she could come with us, and minutes later we were in the Marshmallow, heading to the Burrito Bowl.

"Devin, Dad said we could have lunch at the Burger Hut while you're eating burritos," Maisie called from the front of the van. "Burritos are gross!"

Jamie and I were sitting in the very back row. It was actually hard to get back there; you really had to worm your way into those seats, but whenever I had a friend in the car with me, we always sat there. At least that way we could get a little privacy to talk, without Maisie being right next to us. Usually it was Jessi and me crammed next to each other. Today Jessi had caught a ride with Mirabelle.

"Good for you!" I called back. I looked at Jamie and shrugged. "Maisie's a picky eater," I explained.

"Not my little sister," Jamie said. "She'll eat anything that doesn't eat her first!"

I laughed. That was funny. And not like the Jamie I knew.

"Hey, wait," I said. "Isn't your sister a ballerina? I thought most dancers just nibble on lettuce and stuff like that."

Jamie laughed. "Not Jodi. She's like a human garbage can. She'll devour whatever you put in front of her." Suddenly Jamie's eyes narrowed as she glared at me, all traces of a smile gone from her face. "Wait a second. How did you know my sister is a dancer? Have you been talking to Mirabelle?"

I felt my palms begin to sweat. Jamie looked mad! I didn't want her to think we'd been talking about her behind her back. We *had been* talking about her, but it hadn't been in a mean way.

Before I could answer, she crossed her arms and turned her head away from me, looking out the window. "So this is some kind of pity invitation, huh? I should have known."

"Jamie, no, it's not like that," I tried to explain, but Jamie just stared out the window, not turning her head.

I sighed quietly. To be honest, I did feel sorry for Jamie. That was part of the reason why I'd invited her. Nobody deserved to miss out on celebrating our team's win. I didn't think it was fair that Jamie's parents couldn't understand that.

Oh well, I thought. At least I had tried, and we'd managed to have a real conversation for about two and a half seconds. I wished I hadn't mentioned her sister.

Luckily, Maisie helped ease the awkwardness of the situation. "Jamie," she called into the back. "Do you have a dog? Because I really want one!"

"No, Maisie," Jamie answered her. "My parents say it's too much work, so we've never had one."

"That's what my parents say too!" Maisie grumbled. "But I would walk it every day, and feed it, and it could sleep in bed with me at night too."

Usually I got annoyed when Maisie tried to take over

the conversation when I had a friend around. Today I was relieved. Jamie uncrossed her arms and seemed to thaw out a bit, and I felt better. I didn't want Jamie to be uncomfortable. I silently thought, *Thank you* as Maisie chatted on about wanting a dog, her latest obsession.

When we pulled up in front of the Burrito Bowl, as Jamie and I wormed our way out of the backseats, Maisie gave Jamie a big smile and said "Woof!"

Jamie shook her head and started laughing. Again, I felt grateful to my little sister for lightening the mood.

Most of the Griffons were already inside the restaurant and had pulled tables together in the back, saving enough seats for all of us. Jamie and I went up to order our food. The guy taking the orders was pretty cute, and I felt really dorky asking for the Cluck-cluck-tacular Chicken Burrito Bowl, but he didn't seem to notice. I guessed he was used to it.

I met up with Jessi at the soda machine. It was this really cool one where you could pick from what seemed like hundreds of different flavors. We weren't allowed soda at home. My mom called it poison. But I decided I needed a treat after our win. So I started mixing a bunch of different flavors of soda in the same cup.

"Raspberry cola, fruit punch, and supersour limeade?" Jessi watched, wrinkling her nose. "Yuck."

I tasted it and made a face. Yuck was right. It actually did taste like poison! I dumped it out and started my soda experiment over again.

"So how'd it go?" Jessi asked as she shot a glance at Jamie, who was sitting at the Griffons' table.

I sighed. "Pretty good, until I ruined it by asking about her sister and she got suspicious and accused me of inviting her out of pity."

Jessi shook her head. "Devin, I don't know why you're bothering."

"We're all in this together, Jessi. We're a team," I reminded her. "And Jamie should be part of celebrating our win. We are going to the championships, after all!"

"Yes we are!" Jessi cheered. "We did it!"

"Did you hear yet about the Gators game?" I asked, curious as to who we'd be facing in the finals.

"I texted Zoe, Frida, and Emma, but they didn't reply yet," Jessi said. "I guess we'll find out soon!"

I decided to stick with a mix of cherry vanilla cola and root beer. I took a sip. It was delicious.

Everyone was chatting excitedly as we sat down to eat. "It's getting rowdy in here!" I said above the din.

"Rowdy?" Kristin asked. "You haven't seen anything yet!" She stood up and started clapping her hands. "*P* is for 'party,' and *A* is for 'all right,'" she chanted, and soon some of the other girls joined in on the cheer.

"*R* is for 'rowdy,' and *T* is for 'tonight.' *Y* is for 'you,' and you know what to do." At this part, Kristin pointed at all of us.

"Party!" we yelled as we jumped to our feet, cheering.

We were getting some weird looks from the other

people eating at the Burrito Bowl. I smiled apologetically at the couple sitting closest to us.

"Sorry," I said. "We're just super-excited. Our soccer team made it to the winter league championship game!"

They smiled at me. "Congratulations, sweetie," the woman said.

"And we're not the only ones!" Jessi announced. She was holding her cell phone in her hand. "The Gators beat the Gazelles. We'll be facing the Gators in the championship game!"

The room grew quiet for a second as everyone thought back to our last game against the Gators and how it had ended in defeat. Then the silence was broken.

"We'll beat them this time!" Tracey said encouragingly.

"We've got this!" Kelly added.

Courtney chimed in. "We will not be defeated!"

For everyone else on the team, it was Griffons versus Gators for the title of winter league champs. But for me and Jessi, it was also Kicks versus Kicks!

CHAPTER THIRTEEN

After our celebratory meal, my family picked me and Jamie up in front of the Burrito Bowl. Maisie was sitting in her usual chair behind the driver's seat, with a smear of ketchup on her cheek.

"Hey, Devin, can I listen to the new Brady McCoy song on your phone?" she asked as we climbed into the van.

Jamie looked at me. "You're a Real McCoy?" she asked in a way that instantly made me feel embarrassed for liking Brady McCoy. I was no mega fan like Emma, but I had downloaded all his songs.

"His latest single, 'Beat of My Heart,' is great to run to," I explained, trying not to sound too defensive.

"So can I, Devin, please?" Maisie pleaded.

I dug my phone and earbuds out of my bag and handed them to her. "Here you go, Maisie."

Maisie put the earbuds in and was bouncing in her seat,

singing along to herself, while Jamie and I got settled in the back. My mom and dad were in a deep conversation about repainting the dining room, so I knew Jamie and I would have some privacy. I hoped our conversation would go better this time.

"Do you think we can beat the Gators?" I asked, thinking it was a safe bet to talk about soccer.

Jamie frowned. "Maybe if we can take your friend out, the little one. She's too fast."

What did Jamie mean, take Zoe out? I had heard that sometimes, in more aggressive soccer games, opposing players who were threats were targeted with rough play. If they were injured, they couldn't cause as much damage on the field. While I wanted to win the championship game, there were some things I would never do. And this was one of them.

"Zoe is my friend, but even if she weren't, I'd never agree to playing dirty like that," I said, a little heatedly.

"I know. Devin the Girl Scout," Jamie said in a mocking tone.

"You know, maybe I *am* a Girl Scout," I said. I couldn't help but get angry. "But if I remember right, the Girl Scout beat the cheater last time the Kicks played the Rams."

The words were out of my mouth before I had a chance to stop them. Part of me was glad I'd said them. Jamie had tried a lot of underhanded tricks to undermine the Kicks' confidence during the play-offs. It hadn't worked. In fact, it had made the Kicks even more determined to beat the Rams on the field, fair and square.

I braced myself, ready for a nasty retort, or at the very least the silent treatment for the rest of the ride home.

"Yeah, well, it's easy to be a Girl Scout when you've got the perfect family," Jamie replied. "Not all of us do, you know."

"I don't see how your family has anything to do with you cheating and playing dirty tricks on the Kicks," I answered.

Jamie shifted in her seat, her gaze focused on her sneakers. She shrugged. "Of course you wouldn't. You're perfect Devin, who even tries to be nice to me after what a jerk I've been to you. I don't expect you to understand."

"I'm not perfect, Jamie," I said as I thought back to that time right after the earthquake. "In fact, a few weeks ago I felt like everything was coming apart. You saw me and how I was playing. I was going through a really tough time. So if you want to talk about it, I might understand more than you'd think."

Jamie grinned. "Yeah, you were really biting it on the field big-time, Devin."

"Gee, thanks," I said, but she was right. I couldn't argue with that!

"You've got your groove back now," Jamie admitted. "And it's part of the reason why I think we've got a shot at the championship. If I could be on a winning team, maybe my family would be proud of me. Maybe they'd want to come to my games and watch me play."

I felt instant sympathy for Jamie. Imagine having to win to get your family's approval. My family was there for me all the time, win or lose. Once again I felt so lucky. But I didn't want to show Jamie how sorry I felt for her, in case she stopped talking again. Instead I just nodded without saying a word.

"That's why I tried to sabotage the Kicks," Jamie confessed. "Before you showed up, they weren't even a threat. I thought the Rams had a shot at making it to the play-offs. But then the Kicks started winning game after game. And the play-offs started to seem out of reach. I kept picturing myself at the play-offs with my family in the stands, cheering me on. So I decided to try to give the Rams an advantage by messing with the Kicks."

Wow. I was totally shocked. All along I'd thought Jamie was just a bad sport. Now I realized the issue was much deeper than that. Hurting others to try to get her parents' attention seemed like the absolute worst way for Jamie to try to fix her problems, but I still felt sorry for her.

"You should know you're an awesome player," I told her. "You don't have to resort to dirty tricks to win. You've got the talent. Try focusing on teamwork instead. That's what will help us win against the Gators next Saturday."

I waited, figuring Jamie would just call me a Girl Scout again and roll her eyes. Yet I was in for another surprise.

"You know what, Devin, you just might be right about that," Jamie said. "I've tried it my way in the past, and it didn't get me far. I might as well give teamwork a shot."

I smiled. "So you'll do the cartwheels? And other team building stuff?"

"I guess so," she said. "And I really liked going to the retirement home, especially when we got the dirt on Coach Darby from her mother. Barbie Darby!" Jamie snorted.

"Maybe she'll marry someone named Ken," I joked, and we both started laughing.

Although we continued joking around, I couldn't help but feel a little sad. I still wanted to fix Jamie's problem. Everyone deserved to have someone cheering them on. Jessi had been right. I couldn't change Jamie's family. But at least I could show her I cared.

CHAPTER FOURTEEN

"Hey, I heard you guys made the finals," Hailey said, approaching me, Jessi, Emma, and Frida at our lunch table on Monday. "Congratulations!"

"Thanks!" Jessi and I said at the same time.

Then Hailey turned toward Frida. "Steven told me you're in a TV movie with Brady McCoy. That's awesome," she said shyly.

Frida sat straight up in her chair, like she always did when she was receiving compliments. "It was really fun," she said. "You know, I'm having a party at my house the night it premieres. You should come."

She handed Hailey her cell phone. "Put in your number, and I'll text you the deets," she said.

Hailey looked thrilled. "Okay, wow, thanks!" she said. She typed in her number and handed the phone back to Frida. Then she smiled at all of us. "See you."

"Wow, that was nice of you," Emma remarked as Hailey walked away.

"Well, I made a promise to myself that I would always be nice to my fans when I got famous," Frida said, entirely seriously.

Jessi grinned. "Oh, so you're famous now?" she teased.

"Maybe not yet, but it's never too early to *act* like you're famous," Frida countered.

Emma shook her head. "Oh my gosh, Frida, now you're seriously starting to sound like one of the Real Teenagers of Beverly Hills!"

"Am not!" Frida protested. "And if I ever do, promise me you'll stop me. Hit me or something."

Emma looked horrified. "I would never do that!"

Jessi playfully punched Frida's arms. "Don't worry, we'll keep you in line," she said. Then she turned to me. "I've been meaning to ask you. How was the car ride home with Jamie?"

I chewed my chicken salad slowly, wanting some extra time to choose my words carefully. I really wanted to confide in my friends what Jamie had shared with me. But at the same time I didn't want to gossip. I couldn't help thinking that since Jamie had started to open up to me because I had been friendly to her, it might help her if she had some more friends in her life. It would be great if my friends could try a little bit with Jamie too. Yet I knew they didn't feel too kindly toward her, and I completely understood why. I thought that if I could share with them just a little bit of what Jamie had told me, they might be more open-minded.

"It wasn't so bad. In fact, it was kind of fun," I decided to start with.

"Fun?" Emma sounded surprised. "Are you saying she wasn't totally rude like usual?"

"Look," I tried to explain. "Jamie is Jamie. She can be pretty sarcastic. But she can also be really funny, too. And she is an awesome soccer player."

Jessi nodded. "Yeah, I guess I actually had a good time playing Scrabble with her at the retirement home."

"See!" I said triumphantly. "She's not all bad."

"Devin, are you for real right now?" Frida asked, upset. "Are you forgetting that Jamie is the one behind stealing your duffel bag, ruining the Kangaroos' banner, and canceling one of our practices—not to mention that her final stunt could have gotten us all suspended!"

Frida was talking about how Jamie had planned to spray-paint the field with "Kangaroos Rule" in big blue letters before the Rams played the Kicks. Her hope had been that the Kicks would get blamed for it and be disqualified so that the Rams would win by default. But Frida had discovered the plan, and we'd been able to put a stop to it.

I sighed. My friends were right. But I really believed that Jamie was starting to change. A few more good influences around her would help.

"I already told you how her parents never come to her games—" I started, but Emma interrupted me.

"What does that have to do with cheating?" Emma wondered.

"That's exactly what I asked her," I said. Before I continued, I thought about what I should say. I didn't want to gossip, but what Jamie had done affected all of us. The other girls deserved to know why she'd done it.

"Jamie told me the reason she sabotaged the Kicks was to make sure the Rams got into the play-offs," I shared. "She thought if they did, her parents would come to one of her games. That's why she did it."

Emma's eyes got wide. "That's so sad," she said. "I'm going to go home and hug my mom extra hard today."

"That does put a different spin on it, Devin," Jessi admitted. "But Jamie can be so unfriendly, not to mention downright mean. It doesn't really excuse her behavior."

"You'll see," I told Jessi. "She's going to try harder with teamwork. I think you'll notice a difference in her."

"Um, hello?" Frida interrupted impatiently. "Enough with all the soccer talk and Jamie drama. I've got a party to plan and a premiere I need to get a dress for, remember?"

"You would never let us forget, Frida," Jessi said, laughing. "What can we do to help?"

"We need to pick a date when we can all go dress shopping together. And I mean *all* of us." With that, Frida stood up and marched over to the table Zoe was sitting at. Zoe looked up in surprise. Soon she was standing up and following Frida back to our table.

"Everyone, let's figure out a date and a time when we

can all do this." Frida sat at the head of the table and stared all of us down. I thought I heard Zoe give a gulp as she sat down next to me. I couldn't blame her. Frida could be very intimidating when she wanted to be.

"After all, this is the red carpet," she continued. "My picture might be in magazines. Or on TV. I need to look my best!"

I imagined myself walking down the red carpet. The idea was kind of frightening, what with all those people looking at you, taking your picture, and judging what you were wearing. Frida liked being the center of attention much more than I did, but maybe she was acting more dramatic than usual because she was a little nervous, too.

"We're here for you," I told her. "We'll make sure you get the best dress in the world!"

Frida smiled at me. "Thanks, Devin. Now, what about tonight?"

"Gators practice at three," Zoe said quickly.

"Griffons practice at four," I said at the same time.

"Tomorrow?" Frida asked. "Wednesday?"

"Griffons tomorrow," Jessi said.

"And Gators Wednesday," said Zoe.

"Thursday?" Frida sounded totally exasperated by this point.

"We've got practice at three," Jessi answered.

"So do the Gators," Zoe answered softly. She had been sitting on the edge of her chair the entire time, like she was going to bolt at any second. I couldn't stand the tension between us anymore, but I didn't know what to say to Zoe to make it better.

"So how about after practice on Thursday?" Frida asked.

"Where are we going?" Jessi asked.

"Back to Debi's Discount Dresses," Frida replied. "She's expanded and upgraded her store, and she's got the biggest selection around. She's even changed her name. The store is called Debi's Designs now."

Emma groaned. "Oh no! Does this mean she's going to be even snobbier now?"

"At least this time we won't show up all covered in mud," I said. We had gone dress shopping together as a group once at Debi's store before. We'd been looking for dresses to wear to Zoe's bat mitzvah. When we'd showed up after a practice covered in mud (and cheese puff dust, long story), Debi hadn't been very happy. "Give us enough time to go home and shower and change, Frida."

"Seven o'clock?" Frida asked. "Everyone check with your parents. If there's a problem, let me know ASAP!"

Zoe nodded as she stood up. "See you Thursday!" she said as she darted away, so fast it reminded me of how she moved on the soccer field. She sat down once again with her fellow Gators, and I could see the relief on her face.

"Zoe really is taking this competition hard," Emma said. She looked sad. "She just hasn't been herself. I've barely seen her the last few weeks."

"I tried to warn you all that this game would cause drama," Frida said.

"Once the game is over, Zoe should be back to her old self," Jessi said. Then she added: "I hope."

"I hope so too," Emma echoed, her eyes sad. "And we've got to figure out how we're going to cheer them on this time, Frida. Should we switch signs again?"

"To tell you the truth, I'm really not a Gators fan at the moment," Frida said. "Zoe has barely been talking to me, and she won't even reply when I text her. Yesterday I sent her some pictures of some updos I was thinking about for my hair. No answer!"

She frowned. "Since soccer is about sides, I'll root for the Griffons. You can root for the Gators if you want to, Emma."

Oh great, I thought as the butterflies began to do their dance in my stomach. Zoe had been acting really strange already. With Frida taking sides, things were going to be even more awkward, if that were even possible.

Emma grimaced. "Oh, I don't know what to do! I still want to root for both teams. Are you serious, Frida? You won't root for the Gators at all?"

Frida crossed her arms and shook her head. "No way."

"Maybe I can make a two-sided sign." Emma sounded lost in thought. "And then I can turn it around at the half? Or maybe . . ."

I let out a big sigh. I was lost in my own thoughts. What I was thinking was that while I loved soccer, I didn't love how it was tearing my friends apart!

CHAPTER FIFTEEN

"How do I look?" Jessi asked me. "Any spaghetti sauce stains?"

"No, you're good," I said. "How about me?"

"Good," Jessi replied.

It was Thursday night. Jessi and I were standing under the spotlight in front of Debi's Designs. Frida had been very clear with us during lunchtime today.

"Debi almost didn't let me book this appointment," she'd said. "Apparently she has our names and photos on file somewhere. So please, make sure you clean up after practice, okay? And no food residue." She'd looked at Emma when she'd said this.

Emma had held up her hands. "I will tell my mom to lock away the cheese puffs, I promise."

"All right, then," Frida had said. "I'll see everyone there at seven o'clock sharp."

It was 6:57 now, and Jessi and I were too nervous to go in just yet. Then a car pulled up, and Emma and Zoe spilled out.

"Good! We're not late," Emma said. "I shudder to think what Frida would do to us if we were."

"Is she here yet?" Zoe asked.

"I think she's inside," Jessi replied, and then we all took a deep breath and went into the shop.

We stepped into a brightly lit space with white marble floors and a chandelier hanging from the ceiling. On the wall, displayed in chrome frames, were large photos of models wearing fancy dresses.

"Whoa, did it get bigger in here?" Emma wondered, looking around.

"I think the pizza place next door went out of business, and she expanded," Zoe replied. "It definitely looks cleaner and brighter."

"Definitely cleaner," Jessi said with a giggle.

Then Frida came through a door in the back, followed by her mom—Mrs. Rivera—and Debi. I noticed right away that Debi had dyed her jet-black hair platinum white to match her décor. She wore it in a short, perfectly styled, glossy bob. Her outfit looked clean and perfect too: a white sleeveless dress with a black belt around the waist, and black pumps to match.

"Girls," Debi said, her voice flat. "Nice to see you again."

"Debi has picked out some amazing dresses for me," Frida said quickly. She pronounced Debi's name the way

Debi did—de-Bee, with the last syllable emphasized.

"I'll come help you," Mrs. Rivera told her.

Debi turned to us, eyeing us closely. "Follow me to the salon," she said.

"We're clean this time," Emma blurted out. She held up her hands. "See?"

"Lovely," said Debi, in that flat tone again. "Now please, follow me."

We followed Debi through a doorway into a small room with two white love seats facing a three-way mirror.

"Please have a seat while you wait for Ms. Rivera," Debi said. "And please, no eating."

Emma spun around quickly. "We didn't bring any food this time, I swear!" she said earnestly, and in her speed she accidentally fell backward over the arm of the love seat! At that exact moment Zoe had been about to sit down, and Emma bumped into her. Zoe tumbled back onto the white fluffy rug, bumping into Jessi, who bumped into me. In seconds the four of us were tangled in a Kicks pileup!

Debi rolled her eyes and left the room, shaking her head. We waited until she was gone before we all burst out laughing.

"Oh my gosh, did you see the look on her face?" Zoe asked as we tried to untangle ourselves.

Frida came rushing in, still wearing her regular clothes.

"What are you guys doing? Debi is—" she began, and then her hand flew to her mouth. "Oh no! What is going on?"

The four of us managed to stand.

"Well, Emma was trying to show that she didn't have cheese puff dust on her hands—" I said.

"And she was really excited about it," Jessi finished. "As you can see."

We all started laughing again.

"Oh my gosh, I've missed you guys!" Zoe said, giving Emma a hug.

"Well, maybe you wouldn't miss us if you wouldn't spend all your time with the Gators," Jessi teased.

"Hey, I can't help it if I got put on another team all by myself," Zoe said. "And it's sooooo weird that we're playing one another, and I hate it!"

It was such a relief to hear Zoe say what we were all feeling.

"It's definitely weird," I said. "I don't want it to be weird."

"And I know I've been *acting* weird," Zoe admitted. "I don't know. It's like, maybe I think if I distance myself from you, then I can be more neutral on the field. You know what I mean?"

"Exactly!" Jessi cried, nodding. "But that shouldn't mean we stop being friends."

"It's just a game!" Frida interrupted. "That's what I've been saying all along. But you guys have all been too soccer-obsessed to help me with the most important night of my life, and now Debi's going to kick us out!"

"Oh, Frida!" Zoe cried, and she ran and squeezed Frida in a hug. "I'm sorry for ignoring your texts and not being there for you."

Frida softened. "Thanks for apologizing," she said. "And I guess I'm sorry for not being more understanding about your soccer obsession. As insane as it is."

Zoe clapped her hands. "Come on, let's do this! Let's get you ready for the red carpet!"

Debi walked in at that moment, and the look of annoyance on her face immediately disappeared. "Did you say 'red carpet'?"

Frida turned to look at her. "Yes, that's the whole reason I'm here. I'm sure I told you. My TV movie is premiering, and I'm walking the red carpet."

"And Brady McCoy is the star," added Emma, always the loyal fan.

Debi raised an eyebrow. "Brady McCoy? Why didn't you say so?" She clapped her hands. "Come, Frida. We shall get you red carpet ready."

Then she marched out, and I could swear she was humming Brady's hit "Beat of My Heart" under her breath.

We all looked at one another, grateful and a little surprised by how things had turned out.

"It's the power of Brady McCoy," Emma said solemnly.

"Do you think the power of Brady McCoy can get you onto that couch without you falling on your face?" Jessi asked, and Emma gave her a playful punch in the arm.

We settled into the couches, and a few minutes later Frida came out, wearing a short silver dress that went straight across her shoulders. Her mother followed behind her.

"Gorgeous!" announced Debi.

"Too grown-up," said Mrs. Rivera, and that was that. Frida frowned but didn't complain.

Frida tried on a few more dresses, and there was a problem with each one. She didn't like one. Zoe said the next one was "too last year." (And the look on Debi's face when she said that was priceless.) Mrs. Rivera said one was too short.

Finally she came out in the most incredible, unique dress. The top part was solid back, sleek, and sleeveless. The skirt was made of this puffy white material. It was shorter in the front and longer in the back, and there were colorful stripes going across it.

"That. Is. Fabulous!" Zoe announced, and she gave the dress a standing ovation.

"So cute!" said Emma.

"Awesome," added Jessi.

"You will look amazing on the red carpet in that dress," I promised Frida.

"Thanks so much, Debi, and thanks, guys," Frida said. "This is perfect!"

Debi smiled, pleased. "I'm glad I could help you find the right dress."

Frida went to get changed, leaving the four of us in Debi's salon.

"I'm glad we talked things out," I told Zoe.

"Me too," Zoe said. "How about we make a pact? No matter what happens on Saturday, friendship comes first."

"Friendship first!" Jessi and I repeated, and we each extended a hand for a cheer.

"Hey, I know I'm not playing, but can I do this too?" Emma asked.

"Of course!" Zoe said with a laugh, and at that moment Frida came out and figured out what we were up to. She placed her hand on the pile, and then we all lifted our hands into the air.

"Friendship first!"

CHAPTER SIXTEEN

Friday Night Friendship First Yogurt Fest! 7:30 Yum Yum Yogurt!

That was the text I had sent out to Jessi, Emma, Zoe, and Frida after I'd gotten back from Debi's Designs. Our hug fest had given me an idea—a pretty crazy idea, but one that I thought was worth a try.

That was why, on the way to the yogurt place, my dad made a stop in front of a white ranch house in Riverdale.

"Thanks, Mr. Burke," Jamie said as she slipped into the backseat next to me. "My dad says he'll definitely be able to pick me up."

"No problem, Jamie," my dad said, smiling into the rearview mirror.

Yes, that's right. I was bringing Jamie with me to hang out with my friends. My friends, the Kicks, most of whom were still hurt by what Jamie had done to our team.

I knew this wasn't going to be easy, but I still felt like I had to try. There was no way I could change Jamie's family. But I also knew that when you had good friends, they could feel like your family.

When Dad pulled up to Yum Yum Yogurt, I could see my friends inside.

"Thanks, Dad. I'll text you when we're done," I said, and then Jamie and I went into the shop.

"Hey, guys!" I said, and my friends turned. Jessi looked curious. Emma looked confused and sad. Zoe looked shocked, and Frida looked kind of angry.

"Uh, hey, Jamie," Jessi said. "I didn't know you were coming." Then she shot me a look that clearly asked, *What are you doing?*

"Yeah, well, it was kind of a last-minute thing," I said quickly.

"You know, if you guys don't want me here, I'll just leave," Jamie said coldly.

"No, please don't!" I said. "Come on. Let's get some yogurt."

I had to give my friends credit for being pretty cool about the surprise I had pulled on them. Nobody gave Jamie any attitude, but everyone was quiet as we lined up—me first, followed by Jamie, Jessi, Emma, Zoe, and Frida.

Yum Yum Yogurt was a top-it-yourself frozen yogurt bar. You picked what size cup you wanted, and then you filled it with one or more flavors of yogurt and topped it with anything you wanted from the toppings bar. Behind the glass were metal bins filled with all kinds of sweet toppings, everything from mini marshmallows to sugary cereal to chopped-up strawberries.

I squeezed out a small cup of vanilla yogurt from the machine and then moved to the toppings station. I knew exactly what I wanted. Chocolate chips, shredded coconut, and a cherry on top.

Jamie just stood there, watching me.

"Is that all you're getting?" she asked.

"Well, yeah," I replied.

Jamie shook her head. "Oh, Devin. Do you ever let loose?"

"What do you mean?" I asked. Then I looked down at my yogurt. "Oh, well, my mom is a health-food nut, so this is pretty loose for me, I guess. Her idea of a yogurt topping is more yogurt."

Jamie grabbed the biggest yogurt cup they had.

"Let me show you how it's done," she said. She filled her container with orange, banana, and vanilla yogurt. Then she moved to the toppings.

"You've gotta get at least one item from every yogurt food group," Jamie said. "Chocolate. Fruit. Nuts. Cereal. Candy."

She piled on toppings as she moved down the row of topping bins. I watched in awe as she added chocolate sprinkles, banana slices, peanuts, fruit cereal, and sour candies to her yogurt.

"Everywhere else, you get only one cherry on top," she

said. "But here you can do whatever you want. Why not two? Or three? Or four?"

She added a whole bunch of cherries to the top of her yogurt, and then she held it up. "Perfection."

Emma started to giggle. "Oh my gosh! That must weigh, like, fifteen pounds!"

"It does look pretty impressive," Zoe admitted.

"I like your strategy," said Jessi. "One from every category."

"And you're right about the cherries," added Frida. "I always want more than one cherry!"

I wasn't about to create a monster yogurt feast like Jamie had, but I did grab one more cherry with the tongs and placed it on top of my yogurt sundae.

"Better?" I asked Jamie.

Jamie just shook her head. "You are hopeless!"

Jessi, Emma, Zoe, and Frida finished topping their yogurt, and then we got them all weighed and paid for. We found a round table by the front window of the shop and pulled over an extra chair so we could all fit.

Jamie's yogurt sundae was clearly the biggest one at the table.

"Jamie, how can you eat all that?" Zoe asked as Jamie dug in her spoon.

"We've been practicing like crazy all week," Jamie answered. "I've been dreaming about a sundae like this one. That's why when Devin asked me to come, I said yes."

An awkward silence fell for a moment as we all remembered that nobody else had really wanted Jamie there except for me. I was searching for the right words to say to clear the air, when Jamie spoke up.

"Listen, I can understand why you guys wouldn't want to hang out with me," she said. "I'm sorry for what I did to you . . . before."

I saw my friends look at one another, a little surprised.

"Thanks," said Jessi simply, and everyone else nodded, and that was when I knew that my plan might actually work.

"Enough talking, more eating!" Emma cried out, and just as we started to dig in, Jamie's cell phone rang. She picked it up, and her face fell.

"What? But I just got here!" she said, her voice rising. "Yes, I know Tristan has a game. Fine. Whatever. Good-bye."

Jamie stood up. "My dad's in the parking lot. I have to go."

"But my dad can drive you back!" I said. I didn't want her to go, and I didn't think my friends did either.

"I have to see my stupid brother's basketball game," she said.

"You can get a lid for your yogurt," Emma said sweetly.

But Jamie picked up the yogurt, dumped it into the garbage on the way out, and left without another word.

"Wow," Jessi said when she was gone.

"So her parents never come to her games, but she has to go to her brother's game?" Zoe asked. "That is so unfair."

"Way unfair," echoed Emma.

"I knew things were bad, and this really proves it," I said. "Which is why I brought Jamie here tonight. I think I know a way we can help her. . . ."

CHAPTER SEVENTEEN

"Go get 'em, Griffons!" Kara cheered, holding up a sign that said the same thing.

I laughed. "I wish I could fly you out here!"

"I wish you could too," Kara said. "Frida actually texted me and invited me to her party. That sounds like it's going to be fun."

"I'm sure it will be, but I can't even imagine being at a party right now," I said. "I am so hyped up for this game!"

Kara grinned. "It's so good to see you back in your soccer groove, Devin," she said. "You got your school mojo back too, right?"

I nodded. "A plus on my last World Civ quiz."

"It's a sign!" Kara said. "You aced the quiz, and you will ace this game!"

"I hope so!" I said. Then I took a deep breath. "I've got to get going. Thanks for cheering me on."

"Knock 'em dead, Devin!" Kara cheered me before signing off.

I turned off my video screen and took a deep breath. This was it. I was suited up for the game. My hair was tied back in the tightest ponytail I could make. I wasn't about to risk any stray hairs flying into my eyes. My lucky pink headband was firmly in place. I took one last look in the mirror and then bounded down the stairs.

Mom, Dad, and Maisie were waiting by the front door, wearing pink T-shirts with GO, DEVIN in white letters across the front.

"Surprise!" Maisie cried.

"Those shirts are awesome!" I cried, hugging each one of them. "You guys are all awesome!"

"We're so proud of you, Devin," Dad said. "You never gave up this season, even when things got tough."

It meant so much to hear my dad say that, and it made me think of Jamie—and how she might never hear those words from *her* dad. Which made me happier than ever that Emma and Frida had agreed to my plan.

The final game was being held at the field in Los Arboles, the "home" field for the Gators. When the Marshmallow pulled up, it was still about twenty minutes before Coach Darby had asked us to report, but I noticed that most of the players had already showed up. Everyone was full of nervous energy.

I waved to my parents and jogged over to Jessi, who was standing with Sarah and Zarine, the only other

Griffons players who had also been on the Kicks.

"Oh, hey, Devin," Zarine said. "I was just saying how weird it is that we're playing against Grace, Zoe, and Anjali today."

"See? We're not the only ones who were having Kicks against Kicks anxiety," Jessi said.

We all gazed across the field, where we could see Zoe and Grace starting to warm up.

"I miss our sock swaps," said Sarah a little sadly.

We had this tradition on the Kicks. We all wore silly socks to each game—like striped or polka-dotted ones. Before every game we would sit in a circle and each would pass one sock to the person on our left.

I had worn my silly socks to my first Griffons practice, and Coach Darby had not been happy. So there had been no Griffons sock swaps. I really missed them too.

"I have an idea," I said, and I jogged over to the Gators side of the field.

"Where are you going?" Zarine called out.

"Just follow her," advised Jessi. "Devin's ideas are always good."

I approached Zoe and Grace.

"Hey," I said. "Want to do a sock swap?"

Now, none of us were wearing silly socks. The Griffons socks had a pink stripe across the top, and the Gators socks had two purple stripes. But everyone knew what I meant—it was for old time's sake, a gesture to show that we were still friends.

Zoe grinned. "Yes!" she said, and we moved to a quiet spot and sat in a circle.

It was so silly to be swapping socks that soon we were all giggling.

"Coach Darby's going to flip if she notices we're wearing purple stripes!" Jessi said.

I grinned at her. "Sometimes you have to let loose."

Jamie walked by as we were finishing up. She rolled her eyes.

"You Kicks are so weird!" she said.

Then a woman ran up to us, and I didn't recognize her because half of her face was painted Griffons pink, and the other half was Gators purple.

"Coach Flores?" Jessi asked.

"I had to come cheer on my Kicks!" she said with a grin. "And I had to prove that I don't take sides."

"That is awesome, Coach," said Grace as we all got to our feet.

Then I heard Coach Darby's whistle.

"Griffons! Time to warm up!"

We nodded toward Grace and Zoe and then ran back to the Griffons side. Coach Darby had us line up and do passing warm-ups up and down the field. (Luckily, she didn't notice that some of us had mismatched socks on.) While I waited for my turn, I glanced over to the stands.

I spotted Steven and Cody, sitting in the highest row of the bleachers. The Spartans had lost their semifinals game, so it was pretty cool of them to come cheer us on.

Then I saw Emma and Frida in the stands, and I grinned. They'd done it! Emma was holding up a big sign that read GO! and Frida's sign read JAMIE!

Jamie was behind me on the warm-up line, and I glanced over at her to see if she'd noticed. She didn't at first, but then I saw her eyes get wide.

"Did you do this?" she asked me, and I couldn't tell if I heard wonder or anger in her voice.

"Well, we all talked about it," I said.

Jamie looked away from me. "You know I play better when I'm angry and bitter, right?" she joked, and I heard a catch in her voice. That was when I knew that she really liked the signs.

"If angry and bitter works, go for it," I told her. "Just now you'll have a cheering section."

She looked at me. "Thanks, Devin," she said with that smirk of hers, and then it was my turn to take the ball down the field, passing to Jessi.

Warm-ups flew by, and it was time for the game. Coach Darby gave us a pep talk.

"I know that some of you are worried," she said. "You're worried that the Gators beat us once before. But I'm telling you right now, that doesn't matter. The only game that matters is the one you play today. And I believe we're going to win!"

We launched into our pregame chant.

"I!" I called out.

"I!" everyone repeated.

"I believe!"

"I believe!" everyone yelled.

"I believe that we will win!" I cheered.

Then we chanted. "I believe that we will win! I believe that we will win! I believe that we will win!"

I didn't think I had ever been that pumped up on adrenaline before. This was it! The championship! And now that I knew that Zoe and I would always be friends, no matter what, I could concentrate on the game.

So I was a little disappointed when Coach Darby didn't put me in to start. She didn't send Jessi in either. We sat on the bench and watched the first quarter, but I tried not to get too freaked out about it. I knew by now that Coach Darby had a plan in mind.

Jamie, Kelly, and Sasha started as forwards, and Jamie was on fire. She got the ball away from one of the Gators and charged down the field, making a goal attempt in the first two minutes of the game! The Gators' goalie blocked it, but Jamie was right back on the ball. She passed it to Sasha and then got clear for Sasha to pass it back to her. When she aimed for the goal a second time, the ball whizzed past the goalie's outstretched arms.

Jamie had made the first score of the game! Jessi and I launched off the bench, cheering and whooping for her. I could hear Emma, Frida, and my whole family screaming "Go, Jamie!" from the stands. Jamie flashed me the biggest smile ever as she took her place back on the field. She was the only one to score during the whole quarter, and the Griffons were up by one.

In the second quarter Coach Darby replaced the

whole front line with me, Jessi, and Mirabelle. I knew that between the first three starters and us, we were probably the six strongest players on the team, and I wondered what Coach Darby's strategy was going to be.

I was so pumped to be on the field! When the quarter started, I got control of the ball. Right away Grace and another Gator were on top of me. I turned my back on them to avoid them and dribbled to the left, but I couldn't shake them. At the same time I kept my eyes open for my teammates, to see if I could pass.

Jessi ran into my line of sight, and I kicked the ball right between the two Gators. They weren't expecting the move, and Jessi took the ball down the field.

I charged down after her, and Jessi passed it back to me. I saw Zoe rocketing toward me, and I got rid of the ball really fast, sending it to Mirabelle.

Mirabelle took it to the goal line and then passed it back to Jessi before the Gators defenders could steal it from her. Jessi sent it flying into the goal. She scored! Now we were up by two points!

A few minutes later Mirabelle had a shot at the goal. This time the goalie caught it. Then the goalie stood there, scoping the field as she decided who to pass it to.

"Hey!" Coach Darby called out. "That's more than six seconds! Come on, Ref!"

The goalie's mistake should have been called a foul— and given us a penalty shot. But hearing Coach Darby, the goalie quickly tossed the ball back into play, and the ref didn't call the foul.

"Unbelievable!" Coach Darby fumed, and I wasn't too happy either. The last thing we needed was a ref who wasn't paying attention.

The Gators were still down by two points, and they started fighting back hard. They kept passing the ball to Zoe, who did her thing of zigging and zagging past our defenders. She made the next score of the game against Zarine at the goal. I wasn't happy about that, exactly, but if somebody had to score against us, I was glad that it was Zoe!

The first half ended with a score of Griffons 2, Gators 1, so we were a pretty hopeful team as we regrouped on the sidelines.

"Jamie, Sasha, and Kelly, you're back in," Coach Darby said. "Devin, Jessi, and Mirabelle, stay limbered up. I'll be putting you guys in last quarter."

I nodded. She did have a strategy, just as I'd thought. I anxiously watched the third quarter from the sidelines. Would the Griffons keep our lead?

The answer was—no. Jamie scored again, but the Gators scored a whopping three goals.

"Man, their coach must have given them some pep talk," Jessi whispered to me.

So the Griffons were down by one point when Jessi, Mirabelle, and I took the field again: Griffons 3, Gators 4. Coach Darby had taken our defenders aside, and they looked like determined warriors when they joined us on the field.

I was determined too. Determined to score. And I had

my chance about three minutes into the quarter. Kristin, who was playing midfield, kicked a pass toward me that went a little wild and high. I saw two Gators running toward me, figuring it would be a free-for-all once the ball landed.

But I stopped them at the pass. Before the ball could land, I headed it. I had just been trying to keep the ball away from the Gators, but Mirabelle pounced on it and started dribbling it in the other direction.

I zoomed down the field, keeping pace with her. One of the Gators swooped in to try to steal the ball, and Mirabelle kicked it to me. I stopped it as it was skidding along the grass, and then I took it to the goal zone.

"Go for it, Devin!" someone yelled, and I took the cue. I sent the ball flying toward the goal.

It soared just over the goalie's head. I saw her jump for it. The tips of her fingers skimmed the ball . . . but she couldn't grab it. It went in!

"Go, Devin!" I heard my cheering section shout, and the score was tied, 4–4.

It was anybody's game now, and both teams wanted it. The Gators got control of the ball next, and Zoe took it right past our defenders. She tried to score, but Zarine blocked it.

Right after that I kicked a pass to Jessi, and the ball went high. Before Jessi could get it, one of the Gators flew in front of her and batted the ball away with her hand! Another Gator recovered it and started dribbling.

"Hand ball!" Jessi yelled out, and I knew she was right. But the ref hadn't blown his whistle—again!

I looked over at Coach Darby. That hand ball was a foul that would have given Jessi a penalty kick at the Gators goal—and a chance for us to break the tie! But Coach Darby just shook her head at me, and I knew she was thinking it was no use. If the ref hadn't seen the foul, it was our tough luck.

Time was running out. This was a championship game, so if we ended in a tie, we would go into overtime. That missed call had made me angry, and I was going to do my best to make sure we didn't end in a tie.

The Gators' defenders were sticking tightly to me, Jessi, and Mirabelle. One of the Gators stole the ball from me (legally, this time), but I was relieved when Katie intercepted the Gators' pass.

She kicked it back to me, and I was swarmed by Gators again. Jessi and Mirabelle could not get free of defenders, and I was sure we would lose the ball again.

That was when I saw Kristin, the midfielder who had kicked me the high pass earlier. She was completely free. I sent the ball zipping across the grass to her, and she was right on top of it. She took it to the goal line, shot, and scored!

The Griffons fans in the stands went wild. We moved in to continue play, but the ref's whistle blew before any action happened. We had won!

All the Griffons swarmed onto the field, jumping up

and down and hugging one another. Then we hurried to line up to slap hands with the Gators.

All the Gators looked sad, but my heart broke when I saw Zoe. Her blue eyes were filled with tears. I squeezed her hand instead of slapping it. I looked behind me at Jessi, and her eyes told me that she felt sorry for Zoe too.

I was happy and sad at the same time! As soon as the line was finished, Jessi and I ran to Zoe and hugged her.

"You played such a good game, and you scored!" I told her.

Tears were flowing down her cheeks now. "Thanks," she said. "It's just—I wanted to win so bad. But I guess if I had to lose to anybody, I'd want it to be you guys."

"At least we won't have to play against one another anymore," Jessi said.

Zoe nodded. "I know. I think that's partly why I'm crying. I'm relieved. I'm so glad this season is over and we'll all be back to playing on the Kicks."

"And when we're all on the Kicks together again, we'll be unstoppable!" I promised.

CHAPTER EI

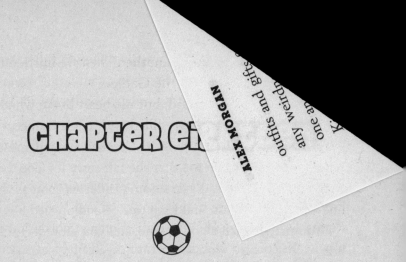

"Do you think Frida will be surprised?" Emma asked as we stood at the door of Frida's house one week later before the premiere party of *Mall Mania*.

"She's going to love it that we all match her party décor!" Zoe smiled.

Zoe was talking about our outfits. She'd had the great idea that we should dress in orange and pink to go with the party theme. Now that the winter league was over, we suddenly had a lot of free time on our hands, and we'd spent much of the past week together. Mostly we'd helped Frida get ready for her party. We'd gotten together almost every day after school to work on the pink-and-orange decorations.

Then yesterday after school, while Frida had been in Los Angeles for the red carpet premiere of *Mall Mania*, Zoe, Emma, Jessi, and I had gone to the mall to shop for

for Frida. It was just like old times, and ...ess from when we'd been competing against ...other was gone. I felt both happy and relieved. The ...cks were back!

"I have to admit, we look pretty good," I said. "And that's thanks to you, Zoe!"

Zoe had helped us each pick out the perfect outfits. Emma and Zoe wore orange, and Jessi and I wore pink. Emma looked adorable in a ruffled orange polka-dotted top, while Zoe had found an orange cardigan. I had on this supercute pink button-up blouse, and Jessi wore a pink V-neck pullover.

"I love the theme you came up with!" Emma said, holding up a paper department store shopping bag. "Shopping chic!"

We were supposed to look like we were going to the mall. Zoe had us wear sunglasses even though it was night. We had them pushed back onto the tops of our heads. We carried shopping bags from different mall stores, stuffed with orange and pink tissue paper. Inside was what Zoe called hostess gifts for Frida. She said that when someone throws a party, you should bring them a little present. I had picked out a box of yummy-looking chocolate truffles.

Mrs. Rivera opened the door and smiled. "You look great! Wait until Frida sees you. She'll love it," she said as we walked into Frida's house. It had an open-floor layout, so from the front door you could see all the way to the back of the house. Leading from the door to the living room was the orange-and-pink "red" carpet.

"Do you think anyone can tell they're bath mats?" Emma whispered loudly as we walked down the carpet.

I shook my head. "No, it looks great!"

The only pink-and-orange carpet we'd been able to find had been fluffy bath mats. We'd helped Frida by duct-taping them together on the back, creating one long carpet. It looked really good!

"Say 'cheese'!" Frida's older brother, Mateo, said. He popped in front of us with a camera, and we had to pose, just like we were on the real red carpet.

"Cheese!" we all said, grinning broadly and wrapping our arms around one another.

We continued to follow the carpet into the living room. Festive pink and orange balloons filled the ceiling and were tied to the backs of the folding chairs that had been brought in, so everyone would have a place to sit and watch the movie's TV premiere. We had helped Frida create decorations by filling pink-and-orange gift bags with tissue paper. We had glued the *Mall Mania* logo onto the bags. They were scattered around the room, creating pops of color.

The room was filled with Frida's family and with kids from school, mostly Frida's drama club friends. I spotted Cody, Steven, and Hailey and was waving to them when Frida came running over. "Oh my gosh! You all look fabulous!" she shrieked as we all got tangled up in a big group hug.

"So do you!" I said as I pulled away so I could get a better look at her. Frida wore a long pink-and-orange maxi dress that swept the floor.

"Mateo!" Frida called. "We need a group picture!"

Frida's brother came over with his camera. "Your paparazzi is here."

We posed for some more photos. I felt just like a movie star too!

"How did it go last night on the red carpet, Frida?" Emma asked when Mateo was done. "Tell us everything. Was Brady there?"

Frida laughed. "Of course he was there, Emma." Then she got a faraway look in her eyes. "It was amazing. Like a dream. All these people calling my name, taking my picture. I even signed some autographs!"

"Wow, we better get yours now before you're too famous to hang out with us anymore," Jessi joked.

"Never!" Frida cried. "I'll always need my friends." Then her tone changed. "There was one moment that almost ruined the entire evening," Frida added dramatically. "My heart stopped. It could have been the worst thing ever!"

Emma gasped. "What happened?"

"Brady brought Star Evans with him as his date," Frida said, and Emma groaned. "When they got out of the limo, I saw that Star had on the exact same dress that I had on!"

"Oh no!" I said as my hand flew to my mouth. All that time spent finding the perfect dress, only to have someone else wearing it too! "What did you do?"

"Inside I was completely freaking out," Frida admitted. "But I pulled it together and pretended like nothing was wrong. When I saw Star, I made a joke about what good taste she had, and we both laughed. But what could have been a disaster turned out to be a total blessing."

"How?" Jessi asked.

"Let's face it. This is my first movie, and I'm not really well known," Frida said. "So the chances of my picture making it into a magazine or onto the web weren't that great. But Star is a famous pop singer . . ." As Frida trailed off, Zoe gasped.

"Who Wore It Best!" she cried. "You made it into Who Wore It Best!"

Jessi and I looked at each other in confusion. We didn't know what a Who Wore It Best was. Before we could ask, Frida continued her story.

Frida smiled as she nodded. "It gets even better." She pointed to the big-screen television hanging on her living room wall. She had it hooked up to her laptop, and pictures of the premiere were flashing on it. Some were from a celebrity news site.

Pictures of a smiling Brady McCoy flashed by, then a photo of Star Evans, followed by a photo of Brady and Star together. Emma booed loudly when she saw that one, and we all laughed.

Then a side-by-side photo came onto the screen of Star and Frida. They were both wearing the same colorful, striped dress. The caption said *Who Wore It Best?* There was a star on Frida's photo with the words "She Did!" on it.

"You wore it best! You wore it best!" Zoe, usually the quiet one, started yelling and jumping up and down in her excitement for Frida.

"And it's all thanks to you, Zoe," Frida said. "The fashion experts liked how I styled the dress better. You helped me pick out the perfect shoes, and you're the one who told me to wear my hair down, not in an updo. The article on the website said that my long, flowing hair complimented the playful vibe of the dress."

"So Who Wore It Best is a thing where, if two people are wearing the same outfit, the magazine picks the person who looks best in it?" I asked.

Frida and Zoe nodded. "Yes, and Frida rocked it out!" Zoe said.

"Star looked pretty too," I said. I felt happy for Frida, but part of me thought it was kind of mean.

"She did," Frida admitted. "But even if Star had won, I still would have gotten my name out there! So there's really no losing."

I shook my head. There were some things about the whole celebrity thing that I would never understand. Maybe one day if I became a famous soccer player, I'd make it into the Who Scored It Best column. Now, that was more my style!

"Congratulations, Frida!" Emma said.

"Thanks! You guys should get something to eat," Frida

told us. "The movie is going to start soon, so fill up a plate and grab a seat."

There was a sun porch attached to the living room, set up with tables filled with snacks. As we filled our plates with mall munchies, Cody, Steven, and Hailey got in line behind us.

Hailey looked right at me and Jessi. "Hey, guys!" she said cheerfully. "Congratulations on taking the winter league championship!"

Jessi and I smiled. "Thanks!" we both said. But I felt a little flutter from the butterflies in my stomach. I glanced at Zoe. Would she be upset?

Zoe was smiling too. "The Gators tried our best to stop that from happening!" she said.

I realized I was holding my breath, so I exhaled before I laughed. "The Gators didn't make it easy for us, that's for sure!" I said, feeling relieved that Zoe was comfortable enough to joke about our competition.

"They sure didn't!" said a voice behind me, and I turned to see Coach Flores standing there. I almost didn't recognize her, because she had her hair in a cute bun and she was wearing a blue dress, and I think I'd only seen her in sweats and Kicks T-shirts.

"Coach Flores!" Emma shrieked, and then there was a whole bunch of screaming as every member of the Kicks in the room ran up to greet her.

Finally we calmed down, and after we got our food, Frida began to flash the lights on and off. "The movie is about to begin. Find your seats!" she announced.

I sat between Jessi and Zoe as the lights turned off and the movie came on. The opening credits played, and a photo of Frida flashed onto the screen. *Frida Rivera as Cassidy*, the caption read. We all started clapping and cheering. Frida took a bow.

It was still hard for me to believe that I had a friend who was a movie star. But even better, I had an amazing group of friends and family, movie stars or not. I had learned a lot from playing in the winter league, including how to be more confident and assertive on the field. I'd realized I could survive a bad game and bounce back, stronger than ever. And win or lose, I was always surrounded by the best friends anyone could ask for, and my supportive family. I felt so incredibly lucky.

And it was about to get even better. Soon I'd be playing with the Kicks again!

TURN THE PAGE FOR A SNEAK PEEK AT UNDER PRESSURE.

My cleats were a blur as I raced across the soccer field, keeping the ball close to me. I darted quickly around the other players.

Was it my speed that got everyone's attention? Or my control of the ball? Nope.

"Devin, you haven't stopped smiling since you stepped onto the field," Jessi remarked, panting slightly as she ran alongside me.

My grin got even bigger. I was back on my home turf, surrounded by my best friends. How could I not smile? I was one of the Kicks again, and we were all together at our first practice of the spring season!

I used to live in Connecticut, where I could compete in soccer only during the spring and summer months. Here in California I could play all year long. When the school soccer season had ended in the fall, I'd been going into some serious soccer withdrawal. Jessi had suggested we try out for the winter league, and I had jumped at the chance.

The winter soccer season had ended a few weeks ago, and even though I'd been a member of the champion team, the Griffons, I had been eagerly waiting for the spring soccer season to start. Now that it had, I was with my friends, playing on the Kentville Middle School Kangaroos (otherwise known as the Kicks) again. As a Griffon I'd had to compete against some of my very best friends. That had been tough. But now we were all on the same side once more. Together we would be unstoppable!

An image of the Kicks sweeping the spring season and being crowned champions flashed through my mind. I pictured the crowd, dressed in the Kicks' colors of blue and white, chanting our team's name. I had just scored the winning goal. My teammates hoisted me up on their shoulders, cheering as we celebrated. I guess I got a little too caught up in my fantasy, because I was taken totally by surprise when I felt something push against the front of my shoulder, throwing me off balance. I fought to regain my equilibrium, but it was too late. I had lost control of the ball.

I saw a girl running away with it, her curly brown hair bouncing on her shoulders as she raced down the field.

"Way to fight for the ball, Hailey," I heard Coach Flores shout approvingly. "Perfect standing side tackle!"

Whenever Coach Flores yelled, she still sounded nice, no matter what she was saying. Coach Darby from the Griffons was always barking at us, whether she was praising or correcting. She was tough, and I learned a lot from her. Yet I couldn't be happier to be back with Coach Flores—except that I wanted her compliments directed at me! (Okay, I'll admit it, I'm competitive.)

Hailey charged down the field with the stolen ball. She passed it to Grace, who was the co-captain of the Kicks with me. Grace sent the ball flying over the grassy field, over the goalie's head, and into the net. Everyone clapped and cheered.

"Go, new girl!" Maya, one of the eighth-grade players, yelled. Hailey was a new student at Kentville Middle School and new to the Kicks, too. She was a seventh grader, like me and my best friends on the team—Jessi, Zoe, Emma, and Frida.

"Her name is Hailey," Jessi called to Maya, her hands on her hips. "And something tells me you won't forget it."

As we switched sides to continue our practice game, Jessi gave me a knowing grin. "She's going to give you a run for your money, Devin," she teased.

"That's why I encouraged Hailey to join," I replied. "I want the Kicks to be the best they can be!"

Yet even as I said this to Jessi, I felt a pang of jealousy rise up inside me. My friends knew I was competitive too. They also knew that I ate, slept, and breathed soccer. I did want our entire team to be the strongest it could be, yet part of me wanted to be the strongest of the strong. Was that so terrible?

The ball was in play, so I didn't have time to dwell on

Hailey or anything else. The other team in our practice game had control of the ball. Brianna raced toward our goal, her blond hair flying behind her. Frida, a defender, stood between Brianna and the goal. While Brianna drew closer, Frida stood gazing up at the sky, completely oblivious to what was happening.

Giselle, the other defender closest to Frida, yelled in frustration. "Frida! Look alive!"

At the sound of her name, Frida turned her head from the clouds back to the field. It was too late. Brianna was in striking distance. Giselle rushed in to descend on her, but Brianna quickly took her shot. Our team's goalie, Emma, dove to catch the ball, but she missed. It hit the back of the net, hard.

Jessi looked at me, one eyebrow arched questioningly. "Frida's head was totally somewhere else," she said. "Maybe back on the movie set?"

Frida was a good soccer player and an even better actor. She had recently had a starring role in the TV movie *Mall Mania* with teen pop star Brady McCoy. Impressive, right? When I'd lived in Connecticut, I hadn't known anybody who was a TV star. It was just one of the many ways life was different in California, like mild winters and having to always be careful to conserve water. An actor friend was by far the most glamorous thing about living in Cali, although I enjoyed being able to wear flip-flops pretty much year round too.

I shrugged. We all had our bad moments on the soccer

field. Frida being inattentive at a practice wasn't the end of the world.

"She'll shake it off," I said. "It's only the first practice of the season. Maybe she's just rusty because she didn't play in winter league, like the rest of us."

But Frida didn't shake it off. After our scrimmage Coach Flores had us work on a simple passing and receiving drill. When Emma tried to pass the ball to her, Frida was looking up at the sky again.

"Oops, Frida!" Emma said in that cheerful way she had. "Maybe I overshot that."

Jessi gave me a pointed look. We all knew Emma had been on target. Frida hadn't been paying attention again.

When Frida passed the ball to Zoe, it went far and wide. It was nowhere near Zoe. Actually, it was nowhere near anyone else, either. Frida, who was usually very dramatic and expressive, was very quiet. After each mistake she made, she looked at the ground or up at the sky. She didn't react at all. Maybe Jessi was right and something was up with Frida.

Frida continued blundering her way through practice. After Coach blew the final whistle, Jessi, Zoe, Emma, and I ran up to her.

"Is everything okay, Frida?" Emma asked. She put a hand on Frida's shoulder, and I noticed that Emma seemed even taller than usual. She must have had a growth spurt over the winter.

Zoe peered out from underneath her strawberry-blond bangs. "Yeah, is anything wrong?"

In the beginning of the school year, Frida hadn't wanted to play soccer, but her mom had made her. After we gave Frida the idea to imagine she was playing a different character in each game, Frida began to love soccer as much as the rest of us. She pretended to be everything from a fairy princess to a military commander to a space alien. Not only did it help Frida play better, but it made the games much more fun for the rest of us. I'll never forget the looks on the opposing team's faces when she yelled at them, "Surrender, earthlings!" We all still laughed about that.

But today Frida wasn't laughing. She didn't seem angry. Or upset. She was just . . . quiet. Which was really weird for Frida.

"Nothing's wrong," Frida said in a quiet, mousy voice that was very un-Frida-like. She shrugged. "It's nothing."

We all exchanged worried glances as Frida turned away from us and jogged back toward the locker rooms.

Emma's brown eyes got big with concern. "What's up with Frida?"

Zoe frowned. "Do you think she doesn't want to play anymore now that she's a famous actor?"

I hadn't thought about that. Frida had chosen acting over playing in the winter league. If it had been me, I would never have given up soccer for anything, even to star in a movie. It just went to show that even though we were all Kicks, we were all different. Zoe loved fashion and had dreams of being a designer one day, but she was just as competitive as I was when it came to soccer. She was one of the first friends I'd made after I'd moved here from Connecticut, but during the winter season she'd been on a different team, the Gators. When the Gators had faced off against the Griffons for the championship, it had put a lot of stress on our friendship. We worked through it, though. And now, thankfully, we were better friends than ever.

With the Kicks finally back together, the thought that Frida might quit was stressing me out. But I didn't want to start panicking yet.

"Are we still on for your house this Saturday, Jessi?" I asked.

Jessi nodded. "You bet! My mom is even letting me pick out total junk food snacks. I know she feels guilty about making me give up my bedroom, so I can ask her for just about anything right now and she says yes."

"That'll probably stop once your new baby brother or sister comes around," Zoe said.

Jessi's eyes narrowed. "What did I tell you? Do not say the B word, please. I have four more months of peace, and I want to enjoy them."

Emma laughed. "Well, at least we know what's bugging you, Jessi. Too bad we don't know what's up with Frida."

"It's pretty obvious that Frida doesn't want to talk about whatever is bothering her now," I said. "Maybe whatever it is will have blown over by Saturday. If not, we'll talk to her then and figure out what's going on."

"And how we can help her," Zoe added.

That was exactly what I loved about my Kicks friends.

We definitely had each other's backs, both on and off the soccer field. I was so psyched to be back, and couldn't wait for the season to begin.

Grace started clapping her hands loudly. "Great first practice, everyone. This is going to be an amazing season. Let's sound off!"

All of the remaining Kicks quickly formed a circle.

"I don't know but I've been told!" Grace began.

"I don't know but I've been told!" we repeated.

"This year the Kicks will grab the gold!" she shouted.

"This year the Kicks will grab the gold!"

"No one can beat us on the field!"

"No one can beat us on the field!"

"And when we play, we never yield!"

"And when we play, we never yield!"

"Sound off!

"One, two!"

"Sound off!"

"Three, four!"

Then we all cheered together. "Sound off. One, two, three, four—sound off!"

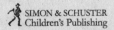

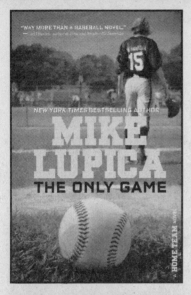
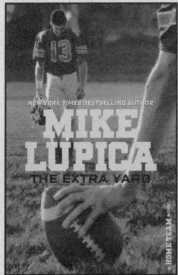
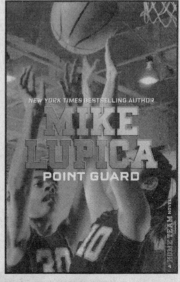

Join Megan, Cassidy, Emma, and Jess as they experience the ups and downs of middle school along with their favorite classic literary characters!

Welcome to Flinkwater, Iowa, the home of ACPOD,
the largest manufacturer of Articulated Computerized
Peripheral Devices in the world....

National Book Award winner Pete Hautman gets geeky
with these hilariously tongue-in-cheek novels.